How it a

Lo Lambert rarely found time to contemplate physics—much less the big bang and relativity theories of Albert Einstein. But hadn't the white-haired genius believed that time could actually bend?

"Dammit," Lo swore under her breath, "time doesn't even have to bend that *far*."

She just wanted to turn back the clock five measly minutes—to when she wasn't yet a fugitive from the law. Or at least to when she hadn't known she was a fugitive. And to when Sheldon Ferris hadn't broken her heart.

She was no longer a successful Wall Street executive. Sheldon had set her up to take the rap for him.

She had to move—somewhere, anywhere. Baggage claim and ground transportation were up ahead. Drivers in dark suits formed a semicircle and proffered large white cards bearing printed names. When Lo's eyes landed on her own name, she jumped as if she'd been goosed by an invisible hand. She couldn't admit who she was!

Another sign. The name Max Tremaine was scrawled across it in black.

Her own driver was eyeing her. "You Loraine Lambert?"

"Max," Lo said on impulse. "I'm, er, Max*ine* Tremaine."

Dear Reader,

The first important thing you have to do this month is to flip to the back of this book and fill out the Let's Celebrate sweepstakes entry, then relax and enjoy another good dose of love and laughter!

Popular Jule McBride's debut novel received the *Romantic Times* Reviewer's Choice Award for "best first series romance." Ever since, she has continued to pen heartwarming love stories that have met with strong reviews and made repeated appearances on romance bestseller lists. A recent nominee for a *Romantic Times* award for "career achievement in the category of Love & Laughter" Jule was a natural for Love & Laughter! And I have to admit that when I told her I really wanted a mistaken-identity book, Jule really impressed me with her twist—a pregnant woman who takes over a man's identity!

Trish Jensen is a wonderful new find. Let me quote from the Genie Romance And Women's Fiction Exchange: "Fans of romantic comedy will be delighted to discover new author Trish Jensen, sure to become one of the genre's brightest stars. In her debut novel, Ms. Jensen's sparkling prose mixes love and laughter in an unbeatable combination of wacky situations, off-beat humor and wonderfully memorable characters. I chuckled, I giggled, I laughed out loud…and I hated to see it end. I want more Trish Jensen stories and I want them now!"

Have fun!

Malle Vallik

Malle Vallik
Associate Senior Editor

WHO'S BEEN SLEEPING IN MY BED?

Jule McBride

Harlequin Books

TORONTO • NEW YORK • LONDON
AMSTERDAM • PARIS • SYDNEY • HAMBURG
STOCKHOLM • ATHENS • TOKYO • MILAN
MADRID • WARSAW • BUDAPEST • AUCKLAND

ISBN 0-373-44023-5

WHO'S BEEN SLEEPING IN MY BED?

Copyright © 1997 by Julianne Randolph Moore

A funny thing happened...

I love to write comedy because weird things always happen to me. I remember, in first grade, bundling up in my little red coat for recess—only to discover my hem hit my ankles, my arms were swallowed and my belt dragged the ground. Doing the logical thing, I fled home, convinced I was shrinking. (Mom's sleuthing—she was a great solver of such conundrums—uncovered that I'd donned a sixth grader's identical coat.) Nevertheless, to this day, I remain confused by many of life's little mysteries—as are the heroines I create. Here, when Lo Lambert meets her prince, she's not just wearing his coat...she's using his name, his house and his credit line. Even worse, sexy Max is highly willing to further compromise Lo's precarious position. I sincerely hope you'll be amused by Lo's predicament!

—Jule McBride

Don't miss Jule McBride's upcoming books in Harlequin American Romance. Jule's ongoing Big Apple Babies miniseries (Can anyone resist a baby?) begins with #693 MISSION: MOTHERHOOD in September and #699 VERDICT: PARENTHOOD in October.

Books by Jule McBride

HARLEQUIN AMERICAN ROMANCE
546—THE WRONG WIFE?
562—THE BABY AND THE BODYGUARD
577—BRIDE OF THE BADLANDS
599—THE BABY MAKER
617—THE BOUNTY HUNTER'S BABY
636—BABY ROMEO: P.I.
658—COLE IN MY STOCKING

HARLEQUIN INTRIGUE
418—WED TO A STRANGER?

For John Slaughter, the most postmodern man I know—
for making me laugh and laugh and laugh.

1

How It All Began with a Big Bang

LO LAMBERT RARELY FOUND time to contemplate physics—much less the big bang and relativity theories of Albert Einstein. But hadn't the white-haired genius believed that time could actually bend?

"Dammit," Lo swore under her breath. "Time doesn't even have to bend that *far*."

She just wanted to turn back the clock five measly minutes—to when she wasn't yet a fugitive from the law. Or at least to when she hadn't *known* she was a fugitive. And to when Sheldon Ferris hadn't broken her heart.

She'd been briskly traversing La Guardia Airport's electronic walkways, looking like a COSMO cover girl—listening to the purposeful click of her own high heels and the swish of her trim sea green silk suit skirt against her stockings. The jaunty tilt of her head sent her layered red hair swirling around her shoulders. And, because she was floating on cloud nine, all her luggage—everything from her practical gray garment bag to her small purse and leather briefcase—seemed as breezily light as the spring air.

She'd been daydreaming about Sheldon, and in the fantasy he helped her celebrate the deal she'd just closed in L.A. After their late, candlelit dinner, he dropped to his knees and handed her a ring-size box from Tiffany's. Then he lowered that sexy baritone of his and whispered, "C'mon, Lo, I'm absolutely begging you. Marry me."

Of course, in the fantasy, she said yes.

And then she and Sheldon were married in an instant mental flash…in an intimate garden strewn with arching arbors and domed gazebos and white-latticed trellises laced with vines and pink roses. After the ceremony, Sheldon carried her in a cradling embrace through a tunnel of sweet-scented flowers to the reception, where they giggled, exchanging bites from a three-tiered cake. On the table, pure golden sunlight glinted off the silver script on the matchbooks and cocktail napkins, all of which read Loraine And Sheldon.

Lo's only living relative, Gran, was at the reception. So was the entire Meredith and Gersham staff, who were thrilled to see Lo and Shel—golden couple of the firm's merger and acquisitions department—finally marry.

It was the most wonderful wedding in wedding history.

Except it wasn't real.

It was only a fantasy begun during Lo's long, boring layover in Denver. And now she found herself back in hard, cold reality—standing stock-still in the concourse at La Guardia, numbly clutching her cell phone and gaping slack-jawed at her own reflection in a darkened window. *I'm a fugitive. Sheldon's not going to marry me, and he doesn't care about the baby I'm carrying. The SOB set me up.*

"A bad dream?" she ventured in a whisper.

But it wasn't. And Lo's mind raced back in time again, trying to figure out—step by step—exactly what had gone wrong.

Only five minutes ago, she'd been an upstanding citizen. She was sure of that much. She'd been briskly traversing the electronic walkways of the concourse—fantasizing about Sheldon's proposal, remembering how happy he'd sounded before she'd left for L.A., when she'd told him she was pregnant.

Suddenly, she'd realized that the ringing she heard wasn't wedding bells. It was her cell phone, which had been buried in the bottom of her pocketbook.

Frantically, she'd searched for the phone—clawing through lip liners and stray receipts, feeling sure Sheldon was calling to propose. It wasn't exactly how she'd imagined the timeless romantic moment, but then beggars couldn't be choosers. When one of her manicured nails merely stabbed through tissues, her knees buckled and her breath left her in a whoosh; all that seemed to stand between her and the altar was a fat wad of Kleenex.

Then, thankfully, she'd found the phone. Heart pounding, she mustered her breathiest, Wall-Street-executive-turned-sex-kitten voice and purred, "Sheldon?"

"Trust me, he's the last person you want to talk to."

It was Lo's assistant, B.B., a Long Island girl with a heart of gold and a tendency toward the theatrical.

Before Lo could respond, a panicked B.B. had rushed on. "It's the end of the world here. Armageddon. And you're dead meat, Lo. I mean *total* dead meat."

"That promising?" Lo managed to ask.

"Just listen." B.B.'s voice had dropped to a conspiratorial whisper. "Do you remember how you and Sheldon handled the acquisition of Dreamy Diapers by Nice Nappies last month—and how shocked everybody was when Nice shut Dreamy's down? Well, now the SEC—that's the Securities Exchange Commission—"

"I *know* what it is, B.B.," Lo had interjected, feeling a rope begin to knot in the pit of her stomach.

"Well, they're saying you took monetary kickbacks from Nice Nappies and that you fixed diaper prices against the overseas…" B.B.'s voice dropped, became unintelligible, then rose again. "Turns out, a lot of your accounts look suspicious. So, the NYPD, SEC, FBI and—"

"A real red-letter day," Lo muttered.

"Yes, well, they all showed up. And Sheldon starts handing them evidence—files and disks, phone records and office logs. Then this guy from the FBI gets on the phone, freezes your bank accounts and—"

Lo had stopped dead in her tracks at that point, her legs suddenly too rubbery to support her one hundred and twenty pounds. Since she'd deplaned, two ATMs *had* refused her card. Without access to her accounts, she was flat broke.

"I ordered a car to pick you up at the airport," B.B. raced on, her whisper turning urgent. "But now, the SEC wants the car number in case they can't catch and arrest you at the air—'' B.B. gasped. "Where *are* you?"

"The airport," Lo admitted shakily. Trying to hold on to reason, she continued, "Look, love might be blind, but Shel and I couldn't overlook price-fixing. I mean, we do all the number crunching ourselves and—"

"Lo—" B.B. groaned. "Sheldon *gave* them the evidence. He said he's been collecting it for months. He said he was so in love with you that he couldn't bear to turn you in until he was one hundred percent positive you were guilty."

"Get me Mr. Meredith," Lo said. "Or Mr. Gersham."

B.B. made a strangled sound. "*I* know you didn't do anything wrong, but everybody believes Sheldon. Meredith was so glad Sheldon caught you that he promoted him to VP of mergers. Sheldon told me to pack my personal belongings after I help the SEC. Then he fired you in absentia."

"But Sheldon can't do that…" Lo murmured. *Tonight he's going to kneel down, kiss my earlobe and whisper, "We're having this baby together, Lo, so you've just got to marry me."*

"Oh, God," B.B. gasped. "The SEC's coming!"

"Okay," Lo murmured. "Don't panic. Let's just—"

But they weren't going to do anything.

Because the line went dead.

And now, full minutes later, Lo was still gripping her cell phone and gaping at her reflection in a darkened window. *Shel Ferris,* she thought with venom. The name fit. Shel—because he was a shell of a human being. And Ferris—because, like a Ferris wheel, he'd sure taken her for a ride. In fact, Lo felt as though Sheldon had just stomped on a magic button in the concourse floor—and sent her plummeting through a trapdoor into oblivion.

Except this was reality. And unfortunately, Lo was still standing in the very airport where the SEC was going to arrest her. Even worse, her fellow travelers were starting to stare. Realizing the cell phone was emitting a loud, intermittent buzz, Lo pressed the off button, then shoved the phone into her bag.

She had to move—somewhere, anywhere. Ignoring her quivering knees and churning stomach, she forced herself to walk. Her high heels—clicking so purposefully before—now chattered like teeth in the cold. Where could she go?

Baggage claim and ground transportation were up ahead. Drivers in dark suits formed a semicircle and proffered large white cards bearing printed names. When Lo's eyes landed on her own name, she jumped as if she'd been goosed by an invisible hand.

Walk right past your driver, Lo. Get a cab.

And keep denying the truth about Sheldon so your heart won't break. But it was impossible. She remembered the many late-night meetings Sheldon attended alone and the mysterious long-distance calls he'd made from her home and office phones.

Yeah, she could hear his voice as surely as if he were next to her. "Something's wrong with my hard drive, Lo. Mind if I download into you?"

She'd laughed. "Download into me anytime, tiger."

Now her temper flared. No doubt the father of her

coming baby had fed incriminating documents into her computer. All along, he'd been fixing deals and setting her up to take the rap if he ever got caught.

It had been years since Lo's parents died, but she'd finally opened up to a man...to Sheldon. And now he'd killed two birds with one stone—pinning his crimes on her and ditching her because of the pregnancy. How could she have trusted him, *given* herself to him?

Just don't think about it, Lo. At least not until you're safely out of here.

She took a deep breath—and a silent vow never to fall in love again. Just as she reached the drivers, she remembered she had less than twenty dollars, and cabs didn't take credit cards. Even if they did, calls made to verify a card might alert authorities to her whereabouts.

Tears stung her eyes, but she blinked them back. She'd been so wrapped up in work and Sheldon that she didn't have a friend left in the world. Cantankerous old Gran loved her, but Gran was still stuck in that nursing facility back in West Virginia.

Near her, a driver said, "It figures. My guy shoulda been here an hour ago."

Lo's eyes slid toward the sign in his hand. The name Max Tremaine was sprawled across it in black.

Her own driver was eyeing her. "You Loraine Lambert?"

"Max," Lo said on impulse. "Er—Max*ine* Tremaine. Sorry, I'm late. My flight...I couldn't..."

The driver raised a bushy eyebrow.

Lo flushed. "I'm just late, okay?"

It was as simple as that. The next thing Lo knew,

Max Tremaine's driver—a heavyset, fortyish guy in a nondescript navy suit—had wrestled away her bags and settled them into the back seat of a sleek, midnight blue Lincoln Town Car. A photo of the driver hung above the glove compartment, identifying him as Jack Bronski. While Jack sped toward Manhattan and Lo's apartment in the East Fifties, Lo riffled through every mental file she'd ever collected on price-fixing cartels, House subcommittees and jail terms.

Not that she had much time to review the files. In less than twenty minutes, Jack screeched to a halt in front of her building. "This it?" he said.

Lo looked—and the shock of what she saw brought on a true-blue, out-of-body experience. She was suddenly floating above the car, staring down at her stunned, mortified self. Not to mention the cops and newspeople on her sidewalk. "Please," she begged, slouching in the seat. "Just get me out of here."

"You a movie star or something?"

Lo craned her neck around and peeked through the back windshield as Jack pulled from the curb. "Er—sort of."

He nodded, seemingly unimpressed. "My orders said to take you to Connecticut, anyhow. That address okay with you, lady?"

Lo mustered her most confident tone, as if she knew exactly where she was headed. "Of course, Connecticut's fine."

But who was Max Tremaine? And how could she explain her arrival at his home? Surely, his flight would come in later tonight. Should she wait on his

porch and plead for the stranger's help? Lo gulped.
Maybe he was married—and his smiling wife would
skip outside to meet the Town Car! Maybe he'd been
gone a long time and his wife was throwing a big
surprise party and—

Lo shut her eyes, pressed the tips of her fingers
against her eyelids and tried not to hyperventilate.
*Why don't you simply calm down? This is all just a
minor glitch in your evening.*

But it wasn't. And when the Town Car stopped
again, Lo found herself staring at a dead end. Jack
circled the cul-de-sac, then growled, "You getting
out or not?"

Something inside her finally snapped. Even though
she desperately wanted to stay inside the car, she
shrieked, "Of course I'm getting out. I *live* here!"

Jack merely grunted, reached over the seat and
thrust a small metal clipboard beneath her nose,
which she took with shaking fingers. As she forged
Max Tremaine's name on the car voucher, her eyes
narrowed. *Haven't I heard that name before?*

She wasn't sure. All she knew was that the man's
uninviting stone cottage was the blight in an otherwise well-maintained neighborhood. Nearby, friendly
lights blazed inside brick houses, but Max's cottage
was dark, illuminated only by a weak street lamp.

As Lo's eyes adjusted, she discerned hints of the
owner's eccentricities, too—weird diamond-shaped
windows on either side of the front door, dark exterior shutters with geometric cutouts, and low-slung,
wrought-iron fencing with skinny posts that squig-
gled. Nature had taken over in a mess of shaggy,
jagged hedges and craggy trees that dwarfed the cot-

tage, and ribbons of riotous weeds curled beside the porch and over a walkway. Rolled newspapers were everywhere.

No wife here, Lo decided. No woman in her right mind would marry the owner of this tumbledown place.

The driver sighed. "Waiting for me to carry you over the threshold?"

Her heart wrenched. *Thanks for reminding me of weddings.* "Hardly."

With that, she grabbed her belongings, scooted across the seat and got out. As she slammed the door, she snarled, "And thanks for the ride."

Then she glanced around as Jack Bronski left her in the dust. Except for the cottage, the suburban neighborhood looked so normal that it broke her heart. Yeah, if only Albert Einstein would rescue her with a time machine. If only she could turn back the clock…

"And murder Sheldon in cold blood."

Less than an hour ago, Lo was just one marriage proposal away from her own little house in the suburbs. Now she was a wanted, unwed woman—with nowhere to turn but a stranger's porch.

It was pitch-dark. Envelopes were crammed into the mail slot in the storm door. When Lo opened the screen, letters and packages that had been trapped between the two doors—everything from preapproved credit cards to coupons—tumbled onto the welcome mat.

Impulsively, Lo lifted the mat—and couldn't believe her eyes. There was a key and a note from a Realtor. Apparently, Lo's mystery man, Max, had bought this place but hadn't yet claimed it. And since he hadn't, she thought, maybe he wouldn't show tonight. A sudden chill zipped down her spine. *But what if something bad has happened to the man...?*

She stared warily from the dark, forbidding windows to the key, then glanced guiltily over her shoulder. Was this breaking and entering? Or just too good to be true?

She had a zillion things to think over. She'd been so sure her missed periods were due to the stressful Dreamy Diapers and Nice Nappies merger that she was a full four months pregnant and totally unprepared. Then there was the matter of the SEC—and proving her innocence. Not to mention revenge.

There was no way she'd let Sheldon get away with this.

Lo stared hard at Max Tremaine's front door. "It's just for an hour or so until I map out a plan of attack."

Feeling decided, she shoved the key into the lock. Then with a swift twist of her wrist, she turned it until a click sounded in the buzzing spring air.

As she pushed the cottage door inward, a droll smile ghosted over her lips. "Hey, Max, honey," she called in an ironic singsong, "I'm home."

And then Lo waltzed inside the place as if she owned it.

2

Many Months Later…

"YOU *SURE* you're Max Tremaine?"

Max was—and he was in no mood. Propping an elbow on his army green duffel, he merely grunted from the back seat of the darkened Town Car. When he lifted his eyes and caught his own intense hazel gaze in the rearview mirror, he barely recognized himself—not the tanned skin or tousled, shaggy, sun-streaked hair or stubbly jaw.

Only his khaki bush hat and safari jacket were familiar. He'd been wearing the damn clothes for months. And as soon as he got home, he decided, he'd burn them. When his eyes met the driver's—a front-seat photo IDed the guy as Jack Bronski—Max finally nodded.

"Yeah, I'm Max."

The Bronski fellow squinted hard in the rearview. "You're *sure?*"

If Bronski kept it up, Max might start to doubt it himself. He fought not to roll his eyes. "Sure I'm sure."

Then, feeling vaguely guilty, he wondered if Bronski was a fan. Since Max's stories for the *New York Times* were most often described as "boundlessly creative and exuberantly human," people sometimes expected Max to be more polite.

Hell, *sometimes* Max was.

But lately he'd been stuck in yet another tiny, war-torn hellhole. And the place had soured his mood. In fact, maybe his mood had soured five months ago—just after movers had phoned to say that the boxes containing Max's possessions were in the new digs in Connecticut. He hadn't even had a chance to un-pack before his editor had begged him to cover a Miss Georgia Peach beauty contest. After that, he had returned to his old apartment for all of ten minutes before he found himself on another flight, this time bound for South America.

He'd written a quick story on the plane about a woman named Lo Lambert who'd been involved in a Wall Street scandal, then he'd wound up covering months of mountain skirmishes—until he'd been thankfully beaten within an inch of his life and left for dead. Thankfully, because Max had been so sure he'd be on the next flight back to the good ole U.S. of A. But no such luck. Until his release last night, he'd been poked and prodded in a makeshift border hospital for yet another month, after he'd recovered from his physical injuries. It had taken that long for a doctor to deliver the brilliant diagnosis that Max was suffering from stress.

No joke.

For months, all Max had wanted was to move into his new cottage. Otherwise, there wasn't a thing wrong with him. And now his editor—overcome with guilt, no doubt—had ordered him to take time off to battle the stress. Trouble was, Max *liked* stress.

Hell, maybe he even loved it.

Nevertheless, he'd already put his boundless creativity to work by imagining a few diversions. Like finding a hot-blooded American woman who was willing to share his homecoming night.

Then tomorrow, maybe he'd shave and get a haircut.

Or work on his cottage.

And, of course, he still had to track down the subslime who'd been systematically stealing his identity.

Last night, when Max returned to the cantina where he'd been picking up his mail, he'd found urgent notices from countless credit card companies. As near as he could tell, a guy had broken into the Connecticut cottage months ago, rifled through the mail, then written away in Max's name for preapproved credit cards. The thief was still using them, too.

Even worse, the fellow had probably gassed up and stolen Max's prized red 1967 Corvette convertible, since there was an Exxon bill. He probably had a heavy girlfriend, too, since there were receipts from women's wear stores named Extra! and Sixteen Plus.

Max had called the cops last night, but between language barriers and bad connections, he'd gotten nowhere. Besides, the crimes had been going on for months, so Max figured another day wouldn't matter.

But now he was home and he'd have to face the music—or mess. No doubt the cottage would be overrun with weeds. God, how he loved to travel, though, he suddenly thought. He just dreaded these homecomings. Even under normal circumstances, they were bad—the dark house, the stacks of mail, cruising the Yellow Pages for pizza joints that delivered late.

Pizza...

No, what Max really wanted was a roasted bird with all the trimmings. It was the tail end of June, but homecomings always made him think of Thanksgiving.

And turkey.

His stomach growled. Hell, even if it *was* Thanksgiving, his folks were in Montana. His kid sister, Suzie, would cook a bird...but then she'd be all kissy-faced with her fiancé, Amis. And that would depress Max further. No, tonight Max was going to be phoning for takeout, then probably showing some cop his empty carport and pointing to a grease spot where his Vette *used* to be.

Vaguely, Max wondered if the cop might turn out to be a curvy redhead who happened to like double cheese, green peppers and olives. Somehow he doubted it. Cracking his window, he stared into the dark at the trees in full bloom. As usual, he'd been on the road too long and missed another change of season.

"You *sure* you gave me the right address?" Jack Bronski asked again.

Max glanced toward the windshield. "Yeah, I'm—"

He didn't finish. His cottage was lit up like Christmas. It looked so inviting that his heart actually skipped a beat. The ever irresponsible Suzie must have been watching the place, just as she'd promised. Maybe she'd even brought him a late dinner...

But no, that sure didn't seem like Suzie. She always promised to watch his humble abodes—then never showed. Besides, she hadn't even known he was returning tonight.

When Bronski stopped, Max scrawled his unreadable signature on the car voucher, grabbed his duffel and got out. Cautiously, he went through the wrought-iron gate. As his eyes adjusted to the dark, they turned watchful. Everything looked so right...that it had to be all wrong. His yard was just too perfect, a showcase of suburban know-how—mowed and raked, with a weeded walk and pruned hedges. Squinting, he tried to remember if he even *owned* a lawn mower.

Then, silently, Max traversed the walkway—his senses on alert, everything intensified. Glancing at the diamond-shaped windows that bracketed each side of the front door, he realized new louvered shutters covered them. Shoot, he'd wondered how to shade those weird windows. Curtains wouldn't have worked. He'd asked Suzie, but she'd merely grinned and offered him a can of black spray paint. So, who'd bought the shutters?

Suddenly it hit him.

The guy who'd broken into his cottage could still be inside. Had he been here all these months?

No way.

Glancing around, Max considered calling the cops from one of the nearby brick houses. Then he remembered that one of his neighbors, Dotty Jansen, *was* a cop.

But what if Suzie had kept a promise for once in her life? Calling the police on his own sister probably wasn't the best way to introduce himself to his new neighbors. If only all the windows weren't either shuttered or hung with curtains...

Stepping off the sidewalk, Max was suddenly aware of the evening silence. Twigs and summer-dry grass snapped beneath his boot heels as he crept around back to the kitchen's Dutch door. The upper half was glass, so maybe he could see inside.

No dice. The window was hung with tasteful gray beads. Not bad looking, Max decided, but he'd never seen them before. The window dressing wasn't to Suzie's taste, either, which probably ran to old bed sheets. At least, he realized with relief, his candy-apple red car was sweetly tucked into the carport.

Ditching his duffel on the back porch, he glanced around again. Was the guy really inside? Quietly opening the screen door, Max gingerly tried the storm door's knob.

"Locked," he muttered. Bracing his shoulder hard against the wood, he got ready to shove his way through if the other guy resisted. Then Max lifted his fist and pounded.

After that, everything happened in a flash.

The door swung open and Max fell through it, into the air-conditioned kitchen. While he struggled to regain his balance, he suddenly noticed the knife. It was long and sharp, its gleaming silver tip pointed straight at his heart. Pretty, well-shaped fingers with red-painted nails curled tightly around the handle, making a vision of Glenn Close in *Fatal Attraction* shoot through Max's mind. The next thing he knew, he was being assaulted—but by the heady scents of bacon and basil. Not to mention turkey and dressing and freshly baked bread—all of which smelled so heavenly that Max wanted to drool.

Instead, he held on to common sense—and kept his gaze glued to that knife. Ever so slowly, the glinting blade lowered. Keeping his body steeled for fight or flight, Max let his eyes follow the blade's descending arc—until he found himself staring at a woman's stomach. And then he inhaled sharply.

Because it was a very *pregnant* woman's stomach.

She's as big as a house, he thought indignantly. Then a wave of brotherly affection made him feel murderous. *Oh, Suzie, I'll kill Amis for you. I swear I will.*

Forgetting the knife entirely, Max stared up at his sister's face. But it wasn't Suzie! And in his whole life, Max had never been more glad he wasn't related to a woman.

Whoever she was, she was an angel.

A redhead, too. And Max had a real soft spot for redheads. Beneath her kelly green maternity jumper, the top buttons of a crisp white blouse were unfastened, making Max imagine the golden fleck-like freckles that probably covered the milky skin of her ample chest.

But Lord, was she humongous. Definitely larger than a size sixteen, at least around the middle. One more second and Max was sure he'd have to redecorate his kitchen…as a stainless steel maternity ward. He was imagining himself delivering a kid on the dining table when he realized it was set for dinner.

For two.

And Max sure was hungry.

Well, maybe he *wasn't* in mortal danger. His eyes

swept over the lace tablecloth, china and sterling silverware his mother had given him. When he registered that a radio on the counter was tuned to seductive instrumental music, the room slid strangely off kilter.

Emotions warred within him. First, he wondered how the woman had known he was craving turkey. Then, still smelling the roasting bird, his stomach growled loudly and he salivated like one of Pavlov's dogs. After that, he felt vaguely queasy, since nothing more than that flash fantasy about delivering the stranger's baby made him faint. And then there was the woman...

Just one look and Max couldn't care less that she might be robbing him blind. But he had to get a grip. She was in his house, cooking up a feast as if she owned the joint.

Max realized he still hadn't moved a muscle, unless raising his eyebrows in the direction of her belly counted. Nor had the woman so much as cleared her criminal throat. Telling himself he'd better take control of the situation, Max lifted his eyes to her face again—only to find himself drowning in the sweetest green-eyed gaze on the planet. His mouth, which had been watering for turkey, now watered for *her*.

Yeah, he definitely wanted to give this delectably curvy crook every possible chance. So, rather than light right into her, he very calmly crossed his arms and waited for her to explain just what exactly she was doing in his kitchen.

She stared back sternly, as if *he'd* done something wrong.

A guy had to admire her spunk. Watching how her

luscious red-lipsticked lips pursed like a school-marm's, Max felt suddenly edgy. With every ounce of his wild, crazy, adventurer's soul, he wanted to kiss her—whether she was a stranger or not. He could actually *feel* how those pursed lips would turn pliant and moist and...

You've been out of the country too long. Still, Max hadn't met a single Hot Lips Houlihan in that damn South American hospital. And shoot, as sweet as this lady looked, just how dangerous could she be?

Wait a minute. Max frowned. Where was the *guy* he'd expected to find? Max glanced past her, scanning the terrain for a malevolent male presence.

Nobody.

When his gaze returned to hers, she merely licked those velvety soft, enticingly bee-stung lips, clearly oblivious to what the gesture did to him. "Look," he began, "I'm—"

"Late!"

Max's ears were still straining toward her voice—it was dangerously deep and throatily seductive—when he fully registered what she'd said. He was so taken aback that his response was barely a whisper. "Late?"

Her head bobbed up and down. And then, as if recovering from her own rudeness, she quickly dusted her knife-free hand against her jumper and thrust it out. "Hi there! I'm Max."

Max—the real Max—made his living by manipulating words for the *New York Times.* But in one fell swoop, this woman had stripped him of all intelligent vocabulary. Finding his voice, he muttered, "*You're* Max?"

When she leaned further forward and grabbed his hand, her shake was extremely dignified and firm. "Maxine Tremaine," she clarified, lowering her voice conspiratorially, as if to say she certainly understood his confusion. "But everybody just calls me Max."

Max found his mental dictionary and riffled through the pages. Still, all he could come up with was, "Everybody?"

"Neighbors, friends...you know."

No, he didn't know.

But he sure meant to find out. He watched in morbid fascination as—knife still in hand—the stranger spun on her heel and charged back toward his kitchen sink as if she were a warrior riding into battle, sword held high. Did she really expect him to follow?

He wasn't sure which he felt more—furious or intrigued. He knew he should grab the nearby wall phone and call the cops, but he kept his eyes on her back, lifted his duffel from the porch, then stepped inside his kitchen again and shut the door.

She shot him such a sweet glance over her shoulder that he was sure she'd get cavities. "I know it's June," she said, sighing, "but I always love turkey and dressing."

Me, too.

"I'll be done in just a sec," she added.

It took everything he had, but he somehow kept any trace of irony from his tone. "No problem."

As he watched her pull a cutting board from a cabinet and begin rinsing and dicing radishes, vague discomfort stirred inside him. Obviously, she was well acquainted with his cottage—better acquainted than he was, in fact.

"Go ahead and put down your bag." She glanced over her shoulder and nodded, making her silky, touchable dark red hair swirl around her face. "I just want to finish our salads."

Our salads? When the heady aroma of bacon assaulted him again, Max instinctively put down his duffel. Stomach grumbling, he decided he'd rather talk to the police *after* he'd eaten.

Unless the woman intended to poison him. Well, he just wouldn't eat anything she didn't sample first. Had his editor informed Suzie of his return? Max suddenly wondered. Was this one of Suzie's friends—someone who assumed she was expected? Maybe she'd introduced herself as Max Tremaine as a joke....

"You're a friend of Suzie's, right?"

She quit dicing the radishes. "Suzie?"

"Er...never mind."

She started dicing again, this time carrots. His mind raced, seeking ways to draw her out. If he could make her talk before he called the cops, he could offer more evidence of her wrongdoing. Did she realize *he* was Max Tremaine or not? "I got hung up at the airport," he ventured, "so I'm sorry I'm late."

Her bubbly chuckle caught him off guard; it filled the kitchen, making him acutely conscious of the pungent scents, soft music and warm, cozy light. He tried to fight it, but his chest squeezed tight. *So, this is what it's like to come home to a sexy woman cooking dinner in a well-lit kitchen. Too bad she's a con artist.*

"Well, your schedule's so busy." Her voice brimmed with understanding. "Besides, my bread won't be ready for another twenty minutes."

"Busy?" Just what did she think he'd been doing? Increasingly, he was sure she thought he was someone else, someone other than Max Tremaine. But who?

His eyes flitted over the table again. Since *someone* was late, would another man show? Max could only hope that some bruiser wouldn't come waltzing into the room anytime soon. Not that Max couldn't hold his own in a fight. He'd only landed in that South American hospital because it had been six against one.

His eyes trailed to a window above the sink, which held the faintest trace of the woman's reflection. He searched for telltale signs of deceit, but her face was so angelically composed that she could have been humming a spiritual. "Anything I can do to help?" he said.

"Why, not a thing."

For the first time, he noticed her breathy voice held a slight twang. Maybe from Tennessee or Kentucky, he thought. Or West Virginia. He was well traveled, with a knack for placing accents, but hers was tough to call.

Well, he just wished she'd drop a hint as to why she was here. Had the guy who'd gotten her pregnant been the one to acquire the credit cards? And was this his girlfriend...or wife?

Max's eyes shot to her left hand, and he hardly wanted to contemplate the relief he felt when he re-

alized she wore no ring. But if *she'd* written away
for the cards, where was the father of her baby?

Max mustered a casual tone. "Anyone else
around?"

She smiled. "Not a soul. But as soon as I shred
this radicchio, I can show you around myself."

Max bit back a grunt of surprise. Was this stranger
really going to show him around his own house?

"I know how anxious you are to unpack."

Somehow, he kept his voice even. "I really am."
Had she been expecting a houseguest she'd never
met? A friend of a friend, maybe? Max's eyebrows
suddenly shot upward. Last time he was here, there'd
only been one bed. Where did she intend to put him?

"Have a nice trip?" she asked.

Max remembered the gunfire and sirens and his
month-long hospital stay. "Just dandy."

She merely nodded. "Would you rather have Boston or romaine lettuce with your radicchio?"

The reasonableness of her tone set his teeth on
edge. So did the fact that she was apparently the type
who ate three-lettuce salads. "No plain old ice-
berg?"

She smirked. "C'mon."

He found himself wishing she'd call him by a
name. That way he'd know who he was supposed to
be and what role he was supposed to be playing.
"Boston's fine."

During the following silence, Max took a good
look around. Unfortunately, the more he looked, the
more annoyed he felt. The layout of the cottage was
simple—a circular downstairs with a living room,
dining room and eat-in kitchen. Upstairs were two

bedrooms, divided by a long hallway. A bath was right in the middle, directly opposite the stair landing.

As simple as it was, Max barely recognized a thing. In fact, from his current vantage point, it was as if he'd entered a whole new dimension—an "alter" reality, where he had two identical kitchens that existed side by side. There was *his* kitchen, which should have had boot-size muddy footprints on the floor and a pizza box on the counter. Then there was *her* kitchen, with brand-new matching pot holders and dish towels.

Not to mention three kinds of lettuce.

When Max peered through a crack, toward what had once been a pantry, his eyes narrowed. Inside was the unmistakable glossy gleam of a brand-new washer and dryer. That meant there was another hefty stack of credit card bills lying around here somewhere. Not that Max couldn't afford to pay them. But then, that wasn't exactly the point.

He sighed. Hell, maybe he *was* having a stress-related breakdown. Maybe he was simply imagining this pregnant woman who seemed to be in his kitchen making him dinner. After all, such things happened to overly creative types who'd been stuck too long in war-torn countries.

But no, this was reality.

At least Max almost hoped so. There was no denying she was the most unusual woman he'd met in a while. And the most beautiful. Just looking at her lush, layered red hair made his fingers long to tangle themselves in the strands. He imagined tilting back her head, probing open those moist red lips with his own and...

It occurred to him that if he played out this charade, he wouldn't have to follow his editor's advice and take time off. There was very definitely a human interest story in here. Even if it was only *his* human—not to mention very male—interest. As Max watched her rinse and dry her hands, he waited to see what in the world she'd do next. Turning around, she smiled—a full-wattage smile, exposing a row of straight white teeth. Her green eyes lit up with the same warmth she'd brought to his kitchen.

Over the softly playing music, Max's damnable stomach growled again.

And she laughed—a cheerful, effervescent laugh. "Don't worry," she assured. "Ten more minutes and we'll eat. I promise."

"Sounds too good to be true."

She sighed. "I hope you like everything."

Max's eyes drifted over her. "Somehow, I'm sure I will."

Then the worst possible thing happened. The phone rang. Her head swiveled toward the wall extension and Max could swear her smile became a little strained. Was it his imagination or did indecision cross her features? He wasn't sure. Because with a quick movement, she leaned and snatched the receiver.

"Hello?" she said.

He expected her to say, "Sorry, wrong number."

Instead, she said, "Yeah, this is Max." And a genuine smile broke through her false one. "Of course I'm coming to the July fourth block party, Colleen."

Max choked out loud. Had this woman, who was calling herself Max, really gotten to know his neighbors? He'd traveled all over the world—he'd trudged through wars and monsoons and covered everything from Groundhog Day to Miss Georgia Peach contests.· Max truly thought he'd seen and heard it all—until now.

Ignoring his slack-jawed stare, the woman merely grinned. "Sure," she continued. "I'll be glad to bring my oil-and-vinegar bean salad and some charcoal. Melvin's providing fireworks, right?"

Max listened to the one-sided conversation with increasing stupefaction. Little Leaguer Timmy Rhys had broken a library window with a baseball, which had upset Mrs. Wold, but thankfully Timmy's younger brother, Jeffie, was now fully recovered from his tonsillitis. Blake and Karen from down the block had decided against buying the Manhattan condo. And the local school board had offered Slade Dickerson early retirement, which his wife was insisting he take.

Max felt reality slip another notch—and the full truth sank in. This pregnant lady wasn't only using his name, she was living his life! No one was onto her game, either. In fact, it sounded as if his unwitting neighbors adored her.

Well, she'd be awfully easy to adore. Max squelched the thought but couldn't stop his eyes from tracing over her again. She was small-boned, probably as light as a feather when she wasn't pregnant. Not that she didn't look just fine this way. But who did she think he was? If she knew Max Tremaine wrote for the *Times,* she probably thought he was still in South America, since his hospital stay had been reported...

Her sharp gasp cut into his reverie.

"Are you kidding, Colleen?" Shooting him a quick, apologetic glance, she leaned toward the stove. As she turned down the heat on a burner, the phone cord stretched taut between her breasts, accentuating her ample cleavage.

Max stared admiringly at her chest, and then his stomach growled again.

"Not Dotty Jansen," she continued. "Well, Dotty *told* me she was considering not returning to the precinct after maternity leave, but she's been so intent on working. She's only due a week later than I am, and she's still wearing a uniform and speeding all over town in that cruiser."

Max's lips parted in astonishment. When he'd bought the cottage, the Jansens had been a selling point. The Realtor said they lived in the brick house across the street and that Dotty was a cop. Had this stranger even fooled the police?

"You think you saw someone lurking around my house?" she was saying now. "That's the main reason you called?"

Max's body went utterly still. Everyone in the neighborhood thought this woman was him. What if she accused him of burglary—or worse? With his luck, Dotty Jansen would shoot him dead before he could even explain his predicament. So much for the welcoming committee.

"Well...there *is* someone here," she said.

Max held his breath.

Then she giggled. "No, I swear it's not a hot date.

Look, I've got to go, but I promise you'll get a full report later.''

Max sure hoped Colleen wasn't the only one who got to hear it.

When the stranger hung up, Max decided he'd better try to ascertain her relationship to the neighborhood's resident law officer. "Sounds like your friend's decided to become a full-time mother, huh?"

She nodded. "Dotty and I have gone through our pregnancies together."

Max mustered a friendly chuckle. "Excited?"

She grinned. "Yeah."

Only years of weaseling his way into no-press zones allowed Max to keep smiling back. He lifted his duffel. "Well, I don't have much stuff."

"Most of it's probably dirty, too." She nodded toward the laundry room. "We'll just bring the dirty things back down. That way, I can wash them."

Why did the woman of his dreams have to be robbing him? "You do laundry?"

"Sure."

"You're too good to be true."

Faint pink touched her milky cheeks. "Well, here I am."

Max's eyes roved over her. "You sure are."

As he followed her toward the stairs, he realized she'd decorated his entire cottage. "Nice place you've got here," he managed to say as she preceded him up the stairs, her cute rear twitching beneath the maternity jumper.

"I've been doing lots of work on it."

He fought not to roll his eyes. "Oh, really?"

"Yeah."

When they reached the upstairs landing, he glanced in both directions. Through a half-open door, he caught a glimpse of the master bedroom—*his* bedroom. A new navy spread covered the neatly made bed, and a sexy, pearl white silky robe was tossed across it.

Turning away, he followed her to the opposite end of the hallway, into the second bedroom. Empty when he'd left, it was now simply furnished, with an antique iron bed and maple armoire. Bookcases lined the walls. Not only had she arranged his books, she'd alphabetized them.

In a corner, he saw four boxes she hadn't unpacked. One, he knew, contained his photographs. The box was just as he'd left it, too—unopened, wrapped in clear plastic and duct tape with Personal scrawled across it. That meant she probably didn't recognize him from his pictures. Yeah, she really did think he was someone else....

Realizing she was watching him expectantly, he smiled.

"The armoire was in Colleen's basement, and Dotty gave me the bed and bookcases. Like it?"

Max wanted to say he hated it. After all, she had no right to decorate his home. Still, if truth be known, Max was none too swift in the decorating department. "Yeah," he admitted.

Her voice skipped. "You do?"

He nodded.

But who do you think I am? He had half a mind to announce himself. No doubt she'd drop into a dead faint if he told her *he* was Max Tremaine. Realizing he'd been staring deeply into her green eyes, he shook his head as if to clear it.

"I'm *really* glad you like the room," she said.

His temper suddenly flared. "Why should it matter if I like it? I mean, the place *is* yours."

Her smile faltered. "Well, you will be staying here for a while."

How long? he wanted to ask. But whoever he was supposed to be, he'd surely know the length of his own visit. How could he find out? And how was he going to keep his hands off her? His eyes slid toward the bed. And then he reminded himself that he was entertaining sexual thoughts about a woman who was robbing him. Not to mention about to give birth.

She headed for the armoire but was still so close that the bedroom seemed cramped. Her perfume filled it—a soft, floral scent that was even more enticing than the turkey.

"Well—" She opened the armoire. "As the agency undoubtedly told you, my ex-husband's gone."

What agency? Max wondered. And was the ex gone as in vanished...or as in dead? "They, uh, did mention that," Max lied.

She blew out a long sigh. "Some friend of his who stayed here left a bunch of clothes. I had the suits cleaned. So—well, if you can use them, please feel free."

"That's so kind of you," Max said drolly as he stared inside the armoire at his own suits.

"It's the least I can do."

It sure was. But what in her story was truth—and what were lies? While Max knew there was no "friend," since these were his suits, there probably was an ex-husband. Babies had to come from somewhere. And she was pregnant but not wearing a ring.

"Besides," she continued, "I never even met the guy…"

A possible scenario formed in Max's mind. This woman had fallen for some lowlife and the man had lied, saying this was his cottage. Maybe, for some reason Max couldn't yet fathom, the man had even insisted she use the name Max Tremaine. And when she told him she was pregnant, he'd left her here.…

Oh, right. Face it, Max. She's so good-looking you're just wishing she wasn't a con artist.

"About your ex-husband—"

She stared at him with a stricken expression. "I've, er, been over all this with the agency. I mean, they should have told you he's, er, threatening me. So far, it's just been phone calls. But I—I *had* to have protection."

It was the last thing he expected. Max forced himself to nod.

Her eyes flitted around the room. "He, uh, didn't want the baby." Her face turned such a bright crimson that Max knew she wasn't lying about that.

"And the closer I get to my due date," she continued, "the more worried I feel. So, I just called the agency and had them send you. I really felt I should have a—"

"A…?"

She stared at him as if he, of all people, should know. "A bodyguard."

Max's face froze into a composed mask. She looked so honest now. Lord, she really thought an agency had sent him to protect her from the father of her child.

This was absolutely insane. He should go right back downstairs and call the cops. But then his gaze took on a life of its own—sweeping her face, caressing her hair and roving over her curves. And Max found himself saying, "Don't worry, Max. With me in a bedroom right down the hall, you'll be perfectly safe."

3

How Chemistry Could Not Be Denied

SAFE WITH THIS GUY? Lo thought.

Never.

Hot-cold, queasy-faint feelings buffeted her insides, and beads of perspiration rolled from her armpits like Sherman tanks. Beneath her maternity jumper, her knees knocked together so fast and hard she could have been dancing the Charleston. Couldn't the real Max Tremaine tell she was nervous?

At least she'd made it back to the kitchen in one piece. She'd nervously stuffed his clothes into the washer, too, and now she tossed her hair over her shoulder, nodding casually at the dinner table, which she'd so foolishly set for two. "Why don't you sit down while I fill our plates?"

Max's grin was devastating—making his amber eyes sparkle and his even teeth gleam white against his bronzed skin. He dragged a tanned hand through his longish, curling tawny hair. "I don't mind serving myself. I'm a big boy."

Was he ever. Lo fought to keep her voice even. "Uh, true, but I know how tired you must be after your trip."

"Actually, I'm pretty wiped out, Max," Max admitted. "I'll take double everything, though. It looks great."

Lo sighed in relief as the man dutifully folded his ample, broad-shouldered frame into one of the kitchen's straight-back chairs. At least she wouldn't have to worry about accidentally jostling him at the counter—feeling the searing brush of his skin, the heat seeping through his shirt, the warmth of his breath as he nuzzled her neck....

Her neck?

Get ahold of yourself!

Ever since she'd gotten pregnant, her hormones had gone wacky, but she was in big trouble here, and ignoring her traitorous physical response to Max Tremaine was the very least she could do. She circled the table—fussing with his silverware and repositioning the centerpiece of flowers. Only after she'd lit the candles did she realize she'd made a disastrous mistake. Everything was so romantic....

And her heart was pounding so hard she could barely think. If only she knew what was going on here. Why was Max Tremaine letting her pretend to be him?

Willing her fingers not to tremble, she started spearing turkey slices. *Oh, please,* she prayed, *make the way to a man's heart really be through his stomach.* Because if it wasn't, she was going straight to jail.

But what in the world was the man doing here?

He lives *here,* she reminded herself. And yet she'd been positive he was still in that South American hospital.

"Hmm." His contented hum seemed to indicate that not a thing was out of the ordinary. "So the basil's in the salad dressing..."

In the perky cheerleader voice that had made her a rising star at Meredith and Gersham, Lo said, "And there's pie for dessert—your choice of pumpkin or pecan."

"Then I guess you'd better go easy on that spinach." Max rested a heartbreakingly perfect hand on his flat stomach.

"But wasn't it spinach that gave Popeye all that strength?" Lo found herself saying.

Max chuckled. "Do I look *weak* to you?"

Lo considered his well-delineated biceps. Then it took two tries before she could clear her throat. "Er, you look..." *Like vitamin E's your middle name.*

"Don't worry." He flashed her another smile. "I fully intend to defend you if your ex comes around."

"Ex?" It took a second to remember she was supposed to be divorced, which meant she'd better start keeping better track of all her damning lies. Upstairs, she just hadn't wanted Max to think she'd gotten pregnant and ditched. "I know you'll, er, defend me fine." *Especially since I'm in no danger whatsoever—at least not from an ex-husband.* She just wished Max Tremaine's close proximity wasn't posing its own kind of threat.

"Count on being safe," he said.

At the thought of counting on Max, Lo's hands started sweating so that when she transferred a smidgeon of spinach to his plate, the serving fork nearly slipped. Darn it, she thought as she reached for the rice pilaf, she'd meant to leave Max's house—she really had—but then one thing had led to another.

Since her arrival months ago, she'd been searching for B.B., who'd mysteriously vanished, as well as trying to figure out a way to get hold of the papers Sheldon had given the FBI and SEC. Now she only needed a little more time. She was sure she could link the paper trail directly to Sheldon and clear her name. In the meantime, she was researching the scandal at the local library.

Of course, a pregnant woman's entire life couldn't be devoted to such activities. She'd been regularly visiting an obstetrician. And at the library, she'd started an afternoon storytelling group for kids. She'd also organized a neighborhood crime watch and a bingo game for the seniors and...

Felt compelled to do something nice for Max Tremaine. So, she'd unpacked for him, getting to know him intimately in the process. He kept everything—boxes of letters, his old *New York Times* clippings, snapshots and yearbooks. Not to mention a lock of hair from his first-grade girlfriend, Molly Miller, that was still tied with a faded blue ribbon. His doting parents wrote regularly about their lives in Montana, and his fun-loving sister, Suzie, had sent a postcard months ago, saying she'd left town with a musician named Amis.

Lo shot Max a shamefaced glance. She'd felt so guilty about snooping that she'd repacked the box marked Personal in such a way that he'd never guess someone had scrutinized the contents.

"Uh...if you keep piling on that rice, there won't

be any room for dressing,'' Max said. ''And I *love* dressing.''

His voice was distinctive—carrying hints of accents from the many places he'd been, and its vibrations warmed Lo from the inside out. She glanced up, hot color flooding her cheeks. With shaking hands, she scooped up the dressing.

''Gravy?'' she managed to ask.

''Tons.''

As she dutifully doused Max's plate with gravy, Lo thought back on how she'd unpacked Max's things and gotten credit cards in his name so she could buy him a few home furnishings. She would pay him back, of course. Just as soon as she had access to her accounts again. She sighed. All along, she'd thought of herself as a benevolent soul who'd come in the night—like Santa or the tooth fairy, or one of the little men who fixed shoes.

But she was a criminal.

She knew that now. Even worse, she'd fallen criminally in love with Max Tremaine.

There— She garnished his plate with a fat dollop of cranberry sauce. Now, that wasn't so hard to admit.

That he'd kept little Molly Miller's lock of hair all these years had sparked her imagination. Then his observations in the *New York Times* about South America had warmed her soul. At first, she'd scanned the newspaper for his articles merely to make sure Max was still out of the country. Later, she found herself poring over them with real interest while she ate her breakfast.

When it was announced that Max's column was

suspended because he was near death in a foreign hospital, Lo had felt worse than on her very first night here—when Sheldon no longer wanted her. And the only men who did wore blue uniforms and carried badges.

Back then, she hadn't yet laid eyes on Max. His work carried no byline, probably because he'd wanted his words to speak for themselves, and the pictures upstairs didn't do him justice. In the flesh, he was more rough-and-tumble, looking as if he belonged on a Texas ranch or an Australian bush safari, not in the Connecticut suburbs. Even the thick golden stubble on his unshaven jaw couldn't hide the sculpted contours of his face. His eyes, which were dusted with sandy brown lashes, were the color of whiskey and glowed like a warm fire. Kind and watchful, they said he could play nice, but that he never let people take advantage.

Lo just wished she hadn't pretended he was her bodyguard. But maybe she'd said that because she secretly wanted him to protect her.... Her eyes landed on his chest again. As she tweezed two biscuits onto his bread plate, her heart thudded dully.

"Thanks," he said.

Her voice was a thin, nervous quaver. "You're welcome."

Once she'd filled her own plate, she stared at the great piles of food. Her stomach was so jittery she knew she couldn't swallow a bite. All at once, she clenched her teeth. *Is Max still expecting the real bodyguard to show up?*

Why hadn't she thought of that? Trying to maintain some semblance of composure, Lo reminded herself that before Sheldon booted her off the ladder at Meredith and Gersham, she'd nearly reached the top rung. If there was one thing on which she prided herself, it was the ability to think on her feet.

"Forget something?" Max asked.

"I, er, better phone the—" what had she called it? "—the...*agency*. While I let them know you're here, please go ahead and eat."

Max's gorgeous eyes surveyed their feast. "I wouldn't think of starting without you."

She melted. Why did Max have to turn out to be such a gentleman? Not knowing what else to do, she strode purposefully across the kitchen. Mind racing, she lifted the receiver of the wall phone, her other hand poised above the numerical pad. Lord, her fingers were obviously trembling! Quickly, she punched in the number for her old apartment, since it was the first that came to mind.

Then she sent Max what she hoped was a guilt-free smile.

He smiled back.

On the line, a piercing tone sounded.

As the operator began announcing the line was disconnected, Lo started rambling chattily. "Hi, this is Max Tremaine. I just wanted to let you know that the man you've sent seems fine."

Fine! What an understatement.

Lo was still fighting the urge to stare at Max's broad chest and shoulders when the line went dead. Her heart lurched. How much time remained before a buzz sounded, alerting Max to the fact that she was talking to a dial tone?

Think, Lo! She mustered her haughtiest, most indignant snarl, praying that Max would focus on her righteous anger, not on the logic lapses in her story. "What do you mean he shouldn't have arrived yet? Well, he's sitting right here in my kitchen!

"Yes, I'm sure he's the right one. His name's..." In a panic, she glanced toward the table. What was a good bodyguard-sounding name? Stud? Rod? Her eyes darted down, landing on Max's feet. "Boots!" Lo blurted out. "His name's Boots...Boots, uh—" Her eyes landed on the stove. "Boots Stover. That's who you were supposed to send." She stared Max straight in the eyes. "You *are* Boots, right?"

Feeling faint, Lo waited for him to growl, "Hell no, I'm Max Tremaine and you're in my house, lady."

"You *are* Boots?" she repeated.

After an excruciatingly long moment, he said, "Yes, ma'am."

Lo nodded as if he'd merely spoken the obvious. "No!" she exclaimed into the phone's mouthpiece, still trying to ignore the dial tone. "I do not want you to *send* Boots Stover. Boots Stover is here! This man just said he's Boots. And if so much as one more man comes to my home, I—I'll never use your agency again! You came highly recommended, too. By...by..." *C'mon, Lo, who recommends body-guards?* "By my very best friend, Dotty Jansen," Lo rushed on regally. "And Dotty just so happens to be with the Connecticut police!"

Making a show of getting her emotions under control, Lo blew out a very long, very false sigh. Then she voiced a cool, "Thank you," and slammed down the phone. Beneath her maternity jumper, her knees started slamming together again.

"Sorry—" She sent Max an apologetic smile as she seated herself opposite him at the table. "I rarely lose my temper. But how do you work for those people? They're *so* disorganized."

"I know." Max shook his head in disgust. "But when it comes to setting me up with work...well, they really are the best."

The guy was a great actor. Better than she was. Lo had to give him that. Well, if he really believed she'd been waiting for a bodyguard, he'd no longer expect another man to show. She only wished she hadn't christened him Boots Stover. Things were bad enough without him answering to that ridiculous name.

Max gazed at her across the table. "Max?"

Somehow, she kept a straight face. "Boots?"

"You okay?"

"Fine."

But she wasn't. That Max was playing along with her was setting her teeth on edge. But it was also creating a heaven-sent window of time. Could she use it to show him she was a nice person? Then maybe he'd believe in her innocence if she told him about Sheldon. She knew Max had heard of her. He'd written the breaking story about the Meredith and Gersham scandal for the *Times* before another reporter stepped in. The paper was still offering coverage, and Lo's name had appeared frequently and in bold type.

As a journalist, Max could help too. But how

could she convince him she was a good person? "Shall we say grace?" she murmured demurely.

Max's eyes widened, but when he spoke, his voice was laced with only the thinnest thread of irony. "How could I have forgotten?"

Since holding hands during prayer was a Lambert tradition, Lo reached across the table, but she was hardly prepared for the way Max's huge, dry palms warmed her smaller, damp ones. Max shut his eyes— as if he hadn't heard her sharp, audible breath, as if the touch of skin on skin didn't affect him in the least. Dutifully, Lo squeezed her own eyelids together. Just as her lips parted, Max's voice sounded.

"Heavenly Father," he intoned. "Accept our thanks for these and all thy blessings…"

"Amen," she said.

"Amen," he said.

She blinked—and found herself gazing too deeply into Max's eyes. Time seemed suspended. Her upper body swayed to the soft, seductive radio music. It was as if Max had put her under a spell. Until the rinse cycle on the nearby washing machine kicked in and he said, "Ladies first."

Realizing her fingers had actually linked with his, Lo gingerly withdrew her hand and picked up her fork. *Even though I'm in his house,* she thought, feeling touched, *he intends to treat me like a lady.*

Or else he thinks I'm going to poison him! At the thought, she winced and the tension sparking between her and Max seemed unbearable. All her unanswered questions were driving her mad: What was he thinking? Who did he think she was? And how in the world was she going to choke down dinner?

She smiled wanly and forced herself to take a bite. He watched her carefully.

Then, as if suddenly sure his supper wouldn't kill him, he dug in ravenously. "Sorry I'm not more of a conversationalist," he said between bites, "but I'm starved."

She shrugged. "Don't mind me. I like to see a man with an appetite."

The way Max's eyes suddenly roved over her startled Lo into realizing he had an appetite for *her*. "Is that so?"

"I thought you were too starved to talk."

"Do you mind talking?"

"You're not talking."

"No?"

She rolled her eyes. "No, you're starting to flirt."

At that, he laughed—a deep, rich, musical laugh. "So, do you *mind* flirting?"

She swallowed hard. "You mean generally speaking?"

His eyes twinkled. "No, I mean with me."

Suddenly reminding herself that she was supposed to be his boss, she said, "Look, maybe we'd better, er, lay down some house rules." *Like how we're both going to sleep upstairs without me losing my mind.*

He laughed again. "Am I making you nervous?"

"A little."

His laughter tempered to a wry smile. "Sorry."

While Lo waited for her overwrought nerves to settle, she watched Max eat, his voracious appetite doing her heart good. Suddenly, she frowned. Because Max had a wide readership, the *New York*

Times had reported on his hospital progress, hinting that he suffered from a stress syndrome.

Was Max confused? Did he think he *was* her bodyguard? But no. Given his appetite and propensity to flirt, he was probably fine. Maybe the writer in him was even intrigued by her.

Lo toyed with her food, then glanced toward the window. In the distance was the Dreamy Diapers packaging plant. It was still closed, pending her arrest and the final review of the price-fixing investigation. Lo shook her head sadly. She'd been forced into constant contact with people who'd lost their jobs because she hadn't paid closer attention when she'd worked on the deal at Meredith and Gersham. In part, that's what had driven her to do so much community work in this neighborhood. Her gaze slid toward Max just as he polished off his plate.

"Something on your mind?" he said.

Lots. She shrugged. "Not a thing. Ready for pie?"

Max actually looked crestfallen. "Dinner was so good I completely forgot. Can I take a rain check?"

"Pie's there anytime you want it," she said, imagining Max coming downstairs for a midnight snack. Somehow, she was pretty sure he slept in boxers and didn't own a robe.

His eyebrows furrowed. "Sure you ate enough?"

She stared down at her full plate. "Jumpy stomach."

"Is it from…"

"The baby," she quickly lied.

"C'mon—" He shot her a smile. "Eat a little more and I'll help you with the dishes."

She smiled. "Bribing me?"

He stared right into her eyes. "Can you be bought?"

At the not-so-veiled reference to her possibly criminal nature, Lo's skin turned hot all over. "No," she managed in a strangled voice. Then she held her breath and waited for him to ask her who she really was.

Instead, he said, "Never?"

"Never."

As she dutifully took a few more bites, feeling like a heel because he was so darn nice, she became acutely aware of the surroundings again—the flickering candles, the dreamy music, the soft amber eyes that kept drifting over her. Oh heavens, she thought with horror, did Max think she'd intended to seduce her new bodyguard? She slid a palm over her belly. She was hardly in shape to seduce anyone... especially Max Tremaine, she reminded herself in no uncertain terms.

But when she lifted her gaze and found him surveying her, she knew instinctively that they'd be right together...holding each other, joking around. *In bed.* Her breath caught. Oh, why had she set the table for two? Judging by the light in Max's eyes, it had definitely given him the wrong impression.

"It's good to be back," he said softly.

"Back?" she croaked. *Please don't let everything be over now—not the soft lights, the music, how his eyes drink me in. It's crazy, but I want this man to keep playing along with me.*

He shrugged. "In South America, everything got sort of out of control. I was, uh..."

She held her breath.

"Protecting a political guy down there, you know."

"That's what the—" she winced "—the, uh, *agency* said."

"Things got dangerous." A wry smile twisted his lips. "But I guess I kind of thrive on danger." He shook his head. "Landed in a hospital, too."

She feigned surprise. "Really?"

He nodded.

Concern touched her voice. "But you're all right now?"

"Yeah."

There was a short silence. And then, suddenly, something magical happened. The lies between them were forgotten. As if responding to nothing more than her genuine, heartfelt concern, Max started telling Lo tales about his trip—about small, colorful villages and hamlets, and militiamen who trained in the mountains. Even though the stories held their share of tragedy, Max somehow found the one germ of humor in each of them.

Lo was sure she could listen to him talk for the rest of her life. He was acting as if he'd been protecting a dignitary, not writing for the *Times,* but the rest was real. Straight from the heart—the people, the places, the emotions.

And before Lo knew it, she was talking about herself, too—about how badly she wanted her coming baby, and how much she hoped she'd be a good mother, especially since she'd lost her own parents when she was young. She talked about her memories of her father, who'd been a physicist, and she even told Max about her relationship with Sheldon, though she didn't mention his name or Meredith and Gersham, and she pretended Shel was her ex-husband.

Finally, she mentioned that she'd lost her job—and explained how that was allowing her to rediscover herself. It was so ironic, she thought as she gazed into Max's eyes. Only by pretending to be Maxine Tremaine had she begun to forget the fast track and remember the family she'd once wanted.

"So Gran raised you?" he said at one point.

She nodded, wondering how much she could safely say. "When I thought things with my—er—ex would work out, I'd hoped Gran would come and live with us." She frowned. "Of course, she's cantankerous and set in her ways."

"She's..."

"In a nursing home in West Virginia." Lo winced, knowing she'd said too much. And yet she felt so compelled to tell this man things. *Everything but the whole truth.* "I—I wanted to make some money, and there weren't really jobs there for me. At the time, Gran didn't want to leave the state, but she would now. I just thought if I—"

"Came here and made good?"

There was no mistaking the hint of irony in Max's voice. She nodded. "That I could take care of her."

"The way she took care of you?"

Lo nodded again. "She's not really fit to be by herself, but she hates the nursing home. And since I didn't want her to worry about me, I never admitted..."

That I'm pregnant. She'd never even mentioned Sheldon, since the stoically religious Gran would have given her countless well-deserved lectures on

the evils of sex before marriage. Lo suddenly thought
back to her school years at St. Mary's with the nuns
and Father Burnes. *And look at me now.*

"You never admitted..." Max urged.

"That—er—I've split up with my husband. So
Gran thinks I still have my job."

"And she can't figure out why you haven't sprung
her from the nursing home yet?"

Staring at Max, Lo wished he wasn't so incredibly
astute. He'd be a hard man to hide anything from.
"You guessed it."

"She doesn't know you're pregnant?"

Lo shook her head.

Max looked steadily back. There was no mistaking
this man's compassion. It was everywhere—in the
candle flames that danced on his cheeks, in his
golden eyes and in his hair. It seemed to surround
him like a soft light. "Well," he said gently, "I'm
sure things will work out."

Lo doubted it, but the sincerity in his eyes almost
made it true.

His laughter broke the silence.

She raised an eyebrow. "Hmm?"

"Do I still have to do those damn dishes?"

She smiled. "You've been so nice, I guess I'll let
you dry instead of wash."

"I'll take what I can get."

She rose. He followed. And soon, with the candles
snuffed out and the lights back on, they were standing side by side at the sink. A companionable silence
fell between them—as if there were no secrets, no
lies.

Max nodded at a pot. "What do you say we save that one for tomorrow?"

"What do you say we just throw it out?"

Max laughed. "A girl after my own heart."

I am after his heart, Lo thought, her own thudding. Months of reading his articles had made her think she could love him. Tonight, she'd realized it was true. Oh, yes, she could definitely love a man like Max Tremaine.

When the dishes were done, Max tossed the dish towel aside and turned toward her. "Guess that's it."

She leaned against the counter and nodded. A silence followed that was too long and too felt. Suddenly breathless, Lo tried to block out the dreamy music. Max stepped a pace closer. For months, Lo had fantasized about Max—and a moment exactly like this. But she forced herself to turn away by barely perceptible degrees. Then she inched along the counter.

Not that he let her go. He leaned lithely, caught her hand and then shook his head as if to say her girlish maneuvers were unnecessary. He wanted to kiss her. She wanted to kiss him. And both of them knew the other one knew it. But she couldn't! She was in legal trouble. Not to mention eight months pregnant and living under an assumed name—*his* name!

Lo's knees suddenly began to buckle. Before she dropped to her haunches, she locked her legs tight. Her mind raced at a million miles a second. What if she seduced Max? What if they married and he became the father of her baby and Gran came to live with them in this nice little cottage...?

Lo, you should be committed!

But what if she *didn't* kiss him? Would he call the police? Would her own friend Dotty Jansen come to arrest her? This time, when Lo's knees slammed together, she could hear the bones crack.

"Max…" Max said softly.

"Hmm?"

"Mind explaining why you arranged for the candlelight and music if you weren't at all interested in a good-night kiss?"

"I…"

She was far too embarrassed to tell him the truth. She hadn't been expecting a soul. She'd just felt lonely. And feeling lonely made her think of the Thanksgiving dinners her family had shared years ago—when Gran was younger and Lo's parents were alive. So she'd cooked herself a turkey. Then, on impulse, she'd set the table for two, just to pretend…

"I did it to foster a good bodyguard-client relationship!" Lo suddenly squeaked, feeling as if she'd won at "Wheel of Fortune." If only Vanna White would appear with a car, so she could drive right out of this kitchen.…

Max's voice was as soft as silk. "The bodyguard what?"

Somehow, the man had gotten right next to her and his head was angling downward. Lo felt hot all over. Scorchingly, searingly, blazingly hot. She could feel the color on her face spreading to her chest, rising in splotches. All her fantasies about Max were coming true, and everything was just as she'd imagined—the heat seeping through his shirt, the warmth of his breath, the…

"Relationship," Lo whispered.

"I think everybody ought to have one," Max returned.

"But you can't get too close to your clients."

"How can I protect you if you're far away?"

The man had a point. "But you're my employee."

"Pulling rank?"

"No, but I don't think you should kiss me. I mean, not that you were thinking about it. But *if* you were..." It was pointless. His mouth was mere inches from hers. Just far enough away that she could see him smile, just close enough that his breath tingled against her cheeks. "Look," she ventured, "it's really not a good idea to...you know."

"I don't *really* know." Max's twinkling eyes drifted over her. "But all night, I've been guessing. And I've definitely been thinking about kissing you."

When she saw the hunger in his gaze, Lo's pulse surged. Dinner had hardly curbed Max's appetite. And she guessed he meant to have her for dessert. Illogically, she considered running for the fridge and again offering him pie. And then she thought of Albert Einstein. If only she could turn back the clock and reset the dinner scene—this time, without the candles and music.

"Honey," Max said softly, "I *am* going to kiss you."

Lo moaned. "But it's just not right!"

"Believe me, Max," Max said right before his lips claimed hers, "this is the only thing I'm sure *is* right."

4

An Object in Motion Remains in Motion Until Stopped by an Outside Force

MAX KISSED like a Mack truck. No warm-up and full speed ahead.

All Lo could do was flail her arms wildly as if she were stuck at the roadside and trying to flag him down for help. "Stop!" she kept protesting. "Stop! Stop! Please stop!"

But the words were so muffled they sounded like "Op, op. 'Ease op." *Graceful protest is simply impossible,* she decided, *when a man's lips are clamped to yours like wet barnacles to a dock post.*

Lo told herself to back away, but Max's eighteen-wheeler smooch had already backed her so far into the kitchen sink that her hind end was getting wet. Her waving hands slapped the counter, then wound up around his neck. She wasn't sure of her motives— if she was trying to strangle or hug him—and she was still so shocked, she wasn't even kissing him back.

Not that the man's kisses seemed to require female participation. He kept right on trucking as if being the only driver on the road didn't bother him in the

least. So Lo did the only thing she really could—
gave in.

And sweet heaven, did it feel good.

Max's velvet lips probed. His playful tongue
teased. And his corded forearms tightened around her
back. The whole time, Lo was breathing in the de-
lectable scents of coffee and road dust and long-
forgotten aftershave while Max's silken, tousled hair
and light golden stubble brushed her cheeks. When
she shifted her weight, his hard, flat belly pressed the
cushioning swell of her own.

Maybe I'll just go along with him for a quick spin,
Lo thought illogically. The second she relaxed, Max
gentled the kiss, as if to say he was awful glad she'd
scooted from the passenger seat and come over to his
side. Suddenly feeling as flimsy as a wrung-out rag,
she reminded herself that she could probably voice a
coherent protest now.

Instead, she purred, "Bet you played football in
high school."

Max smiled against her lips. "Quarterback."

She knew that, of course, since she'd scrutinized
all his yearbooks. "Brains *and* brawn."

He leaned back a hairbreadth. "Which do you like
best in a guy?"

Lo thought of the way Sheldon's criminal mind
had destroyed her life. "Brawn."

Max chuckled. "How shallow."

Lo's answering smile turned wan. Lord, she was
in trouble. Max was so sexy. And so nice. She knew
he was smart, too. She just wished she didn't like
him so much. Not his open, easy manner. Or the

sexy, masculine way he smelled. Or the fact that he cared about the world beyond himself.

"Brawn, huh?" he murmured.

"I've run into my share of trouble with the brainy variety," she whispered back.

"Variety? You make guys sound like garden plants."

"Face it, some *are* weeds."

"And some are Venus flytraps." Max grinned and devoured her with another kiss.

Lo gingerly squirmed sideways. "Look—er—*Boots,* our situation is a little sticky…"

"That's why I'm sticking with you."

There was just no stopping him. The Venus flytrap planted his lips on hers again. This time, the kiss was an obvious invitation to more. Lo tried not to R.S.V.P. so enthusiastically in the affirmative. But the kiss was as sure as fate and taxes, and it felt so right and good…

Until Max gasped.

Lo's eyes flew open just in time to see Max step back, stare at her belly and swallow hard.

"It kicked me," he said.

Lo's hand shot to her belly just as the baby moved again. Bone-deep defensiveness made all the color drain from her face. "It hardly kicked you intentionally!"

Max stared at her. "Look, I was just…"

Everything in his stupefied expression reminded Lo of why they shouldn't be kissing. "I *know* what you were doing," she forced herself to say. "Which is why you'd better stop."

Clearly thinking of how the baby had surprised him, Max said, "It was nothing personal."

Thinking of the kiss, Lo said, "It was *very* personal."

Max's longing eyes now locked on her lips. "Really, I was just surprised. I mean, I felt this thing—"

Lo's eyes bugged. "This *thing* is my baby!"

Max squinted, clearly wondering how their first kiss had veered in this strange direction. "I know that."

She crossed her arms. "Then why were you so surprised?"

"It just caught me off guard. Okay?"

"No, it's not okay." *And you're just like Sheldon.* Given his position at the *Times,* Max was probably a fast-track careerist who didn't care about family and kids. *Or like to be crossed,* she decided when Max's eyes narrowed. Still feeling the cocksure pressure of his lips on hers, she glared back. "A big guy like you has to be *on guard* against an unborn baby?"

"No," Max growled. "I—"

"Please." She held up her hand. "I've met plenty of men like you, so I know exactly what you're trying to say."

Right now Max wasn't trying to say a thing. He was merely gawking. "Men like me? Look, lady, is this some kind of a hormonal thing?"

"Excuse me?"

"Sorry," he returned with measured calm. "I've just read that hormones can kick in during pregnancy. The, er, *New York Times* did a series of articles and…"

Max had done the articles. Lo had seen them at the library. "And?"

"And," he continued smoothly, "I'm sure it's not true."

He was lying. He was right, too. Her wacky hormones had spun out of control. Not that it was polite of Max to mention it. Especially since it was *his* kiss that had made her short-circuit. She'd been such a fool to give in and kiss him back. And now, before she did something worse, she really had to get out of here. She glanced casually over her shoulder, gauging the distance to the stairs. Then she simply whirled around and fled.

"Max?" he yelled.

What he meant was, "Get back here, lady." Not that Lo was about to reverse directions. Not even when she heard the heavy tread of his boots behind her.

His soft curse sounded. "Max? Oh, Ma-ax."

She had to get to her room! She had to think! She'd just made a complete fool of herself. She scrambled upstairs, ran inside the master bedroom and slammed the door. Leaning breathlessly against it, she decided she could kill Max Tremaine for showing up unexpectedly and kissing her like that.

It was all too much.

And now her insides were zinging with wild, crazy energy. It *was* hormonal, of course. It had nothing— zilch, zero, nada—to do with Max Tremaine. From experience Lo knew the miserable emotional episode would pass, but for now, her small body didn't seem large enough to contain all her pent-up energy. If only she could have some release...

Like eating that mint-chocolate-chip Häagen-Dazs in the freezer. Or flinging herself on the bed for a good cry. *Or making love to Max.*

She could, too. Because he was upstairs now—and heading right for her bedroom. Lo's flattened palms glided over the door. Tears sprang to her eyes. She was in such a mess! Even worse, the most appealing man she'd ever met didn't like her baby! He'd kissed her like the devil, then called her unborn child a thing!

Lo took a tremulous breath, wishing there was a lock on the door. Fortunately, because she was pregnant, she'd been watching her diet and taking vitamins the size of horse tranquilizers. Even her hair was strong, twice as thick as it used to be.

So she waddled right across the room, grabbed an armchair, hauled it back to the door and wedged it beneath the doorknob. Then she stalked to the chest of drawers. From the top, she swiped aside magazines and books. Then she hunkered over, pressed her shoulder against the chest and shoved. After a moment, her grunts turned to sighs. Even with her new pregnancy muscles, the chest was too heavy. Her eyes darted to the door again.

Max was right outside. She could *feel* him.

Scampering in front of the chest, she wrenched open the drawers and began emptying the contents. Fistfuls of jeans, nighties and underwear flew every which way. When a see-through blue robe unfurled in midair, Lo's heart wrenched. She'd bought that gown months ago in L.A. She had planned to wear it the night she returned, after Sheldon Ferris knelt in front of her and proposed....

"Are you all right in there or not?" Max demanded.

I'm just fine. As if to prove it, Lo slammed the drawers shut, adjusted her weight against the dresser again and pushed. This time the chest slowly scraped across the hardwood floor—until it hit the door.

Now she was safe.

Feeling relieved, Lo whirled around. The room looked as if a cyclone had hit it. Clothes and magazines were everywhere. Maybe she really had lost her mind. Max Tremaine had sure been looking at her as if she'd gone crazy.

"Could you at least do me a favor and answer me?" he yelled.

What was there to say? Lo plopped down on the bed and stared at the door. Suddenly, the furniture in front of it looked extremely heavy. How had she managed to move it all? She clasped her hands nervously in her lap.

"Max?"

The voice coming through the door was muffled by all the furniture. "Just go away!" she shouted, guessing she owed him that much.

And then the last thing she expected happened. When she thought she heard his steps recede down the hall, she actually burst into tears.

"What is wr-wrong with me?" she sobbed. She knew she couldn't afford to fall apart. But Max's kiss had unhinged her. It was no darn wonder the man's articles weren't accompanied by a photograph. If they were, every woman in America would be spinning through the revolving doors of the *New York Times* trying to get a piece of him.

Heaven knew, Lo hadn't wanted to stop kissing Max—and her baby was nearly due! It was all so wrong. And yet so right. She wiped away her tears. Given her outburst, Max was probably calling the police right now....

Or would he take pity? A kiss like the one they'd shared sure made *her* feel more merciful. Besides, all she wanted was to stay out of trouble, have her baby and go somewhere she could live with Gran.

Gran. Lo sighed. She'd wanted to make her so proud. That was why Lo had put herself through college and headed for the bright lights and big city.

Where you completely failed.

How could she have come so far, only to be spit out like chump change? Because of her, everyone in this part of Connecticut had lost their jobs. Even worse, she was unmarried, pregnant, on the lam, kissing men she barely knew...

And so hungry she could eat a horse.

Her stomach growled, and Max's sexy, rumbling voice teased her consciousness. "Eat a little more and I'll help you do the dishes."

Lo should have listened to him. But no. Now she was locked in her room, where she'd surely starve to death. The shiny white surface of the refrigerator gleamed in her mind. She saw herself dreamily opening the door and reaching into the freezer for that mint-chocolate-chip Häagen-Dazs. She could actually feel the ice crystals teasing her fingertips and taste the cold, gooey ice cream melting on her tongue. A hunger pang squeezed her belly. The baby kicked in consternation. And she realized she was salivating.

Not that she was about to move.

Lo merely stared miserably at the furniture stacked in front of the closed door. Because the only thing she desired more than that Häagen-Dazs was to avoid Max's unnerving kisses.

MAX EYED THE DOOR.

He was sorely tempted to break it down. But then the crazy stranger had already wreaked enough havoc on his home without adding door destruction to the list. He hardly wanted to contemplate what all that furniture moving had done to his polished hardwood floors.

"Women," Max muttered as he turned on his heel and headed downstairs. They'd done a lot of things to him, but none had ever confused him this badly.

When he reached the kitchen, he started searching through drawers and cabinets, determined to find some clue to the woman's identity. Suddenly he stopped and cocked his head. He could have sworn he heard something. But it wasn't her. Shoot, she'd hemmed herself in with so much furniture that he'd probably *never* see her again.

"Fine by me," he muttered, recalling how she'd stared at him as if he were some sort of baby-hater.

He shook his head, remembering how shocked— and moved—he'd been when the baby's tiny kick had reverberated against his abdomen. He'd been kissing the stranger, preparing to edge her toward a bedroom. Since he'd never so much as thought about making love to a pregnant woman before, he'd been mentally reviewing some old articles he'd written on pregnancy for the *Times,* hoping for hints. But it had been so long ago...

And then the baby kicked.

For a half second, Max was sure he'd pressed against her belly too hard, causing the kid mortal damage. But before he could even ask, the redhead had gone ballistic.

Finding no clues in the kitchen, Max ambled toward the living room, wishing he wasn't so tired. He'd definitely rather worry about the mystery woman tomorrow.

Not that he could. Especially since he was so sure she'd really been expecting a bodyguard who wasn't going to show up now. Her angry call to the agency had been too real to be a performance. That meant the woman was in danger—and without professional protection.

"As hormonal as she is," Max muttered, "I feel sorry for any guy who comes after her."

In the living room, the top of his cherrywood rolltop desk was open, exposing a brand-new telephone. Seating himself, Max simultaneously dialed Suzie's apartment and peered into his desk drawers. Just as Suzie's message beep sounded, Max found the motherlode—a shoe box filled with envelopes, articles and receipts. He hauled it to the desktop.

"This is Suzie," his sister said perkily. "Don't bother to leave a message..."

Max came to full attention. If there was one thing in this world about which his little sister was meticulous, it was getting her phone messages.

"Amis got some gigs in Europe," she continued, "and if everything works out, I'm going to marry him right on top of the Eiffel Tower. I just love the idea of throwing a bouquet off of that old thing, don't you?''

The beep sounded.

''You could be in the middle of the Sahara without water, and I know you'd still be checking your messages,'' Max said. ''So you'd better call me back. The number's—'' Max sighed and held out the phone receiver, hoping to find the number. No such luck. ''Well…call information, Suzie. I guess it's listed.'' Then, as an afterthought, he added, ''This is your brother.''

Then he hung up.

Great. A strange woman was living in his new cottage, and his sister was eloping. Max felt torn between brotherly concern and envy. Suzie was still in her twenties and she'd already found her mate. She and Amis had been joined at the hip since grade school.

It just didn't seem fair.

To add insult to injury, Max didn't even know his own phone number. Or have a clue as to what the woman had listed it under. The only thing he'd managed to find out about her so far was that she was an A-list kisser.

With renewed determination, Max stared at the shoe box. The box itself was from Saks Fifth Avenue, which meant his houseguest had expensive taste in shoes. He sighed. ''Way to go, Sherlock.''

Not that the contents were any more illuminating. There was a set of keys Max didn't recognize, and a pamphlet about finding your true self. *Definitely an area where the woman has difficulty.* Max studied some paid bills for an expensive nursing home in West Virginia, which meant he was paying her grandmother's rent. Then he fingered through countless credit card receipts mingled with recipes the woman had clipped from *Bon Appétit*.

One for lamb chops in orange sauce made Max's mouth water, so he gingerly put it aside. Then he wondered why. Was he really contemplating asking the strange woman hemmed in by furniture upstairs to cook him lamb chops? "Yeah, right. And is that before or after you kiss her again?"

After.

Yeah, he was definitely going to kiss her again. She'd felt too good in his arms. Besides, Max loved a walking mystery. And he rarely saw one walking around with such great legs.

"Bavarian peach cobbler," he murmured. He carefully placed that recipe aside, also.

And then Max found a stray receipt from the car company he used to get to and from the airport. Jack Bronski was listed as the driver, and Max's signature was clearly forged. Had the woman upstairs used his car service to get here? Max's frown deepened. Something about the receipt was setting off warning bells....

He shrugged and kept rummaging until his fingers stilled on an old article he'd written about a Wall Street scandal. A source had tipped off Max while he was on the plane bound for South America. Max had broken the story, then a guy on the metro desk had taken over.

It was just as well, too. White-collar crime bored Max to tears. He'd take the overseas beat any day, with its dirty politics, movers and shakers and high stakes. But why were so many of these stories from the *Times?*

Suddenly, Max murmured, "Practically all these articles are about that Loraine Lambert thing."

The former Meredith and Gersham employee had fixed prices and finalized countless suspect deals. A number of people in the surrounding Connecticut area were laid off because of her. Just down the road, the Dreamy Diapers packaging plant had shut down. He glanced over the tabloid headlines that had run in the *New York Post:* Lambert Leads Lambs To Slaughter! Lady On The Lambert! Lower Than Lo?

Both Loraine Lambert and her alleged accomplice were still missing. "I'd sure love to be the reporter who found her."

Max raised a sandy eyebrow. Then he glanced toward the stairs and brought the photograph closer. There was no mistaking that face. Or the layered red hair. Not to mention the perfect legs he'd been ogling and the lush mouth he'd just kissed senseless.

Right before Max's eyes dropped to the caption, he whispered, "Tell me she isn't Lo Lambert."

But, of course, she was.

5

What Goes Up Must Come Down

MAX WOKE WITH A START. He was lying on his back, his body stock-still, his muscles tense. The digital clock beside him said 4:00 a.m. Had he heard a noise downstairs?

No.

But something *was* in bed with him—and moving! Was it Lo Lambert? Max flicked on a bedside lamp and peered around. Beneath the covers, something bobbed up and down, but it was far too small to be a woman. Feeling a little disappointed, Max groggily wondered if Lo was just a figment of his overactive imagination. Maybe he was still in some backwoods mountain village, suffering from stress. Maybe a field mouse had gotten in...

Just as he whisked back the covers, a creature lunged for his throat. Catching it in midair, Max met the gaze of mean yellow eyes. Then the white ball of fur with black markings let out a peep. ''Darn thing can't even meow right,'' Max muttered.

He sighed. Lo Lambert was no dream. Not only had the most wanted criminal in the area helped herself to his cottage and equipped the fridge with three kinds of lettuce, she'd apparently brought a pet. Nevertheless, Max could make swift adjustments—especially since he'd just landed the scoop of his career. He could already see the headlines about his undercover life with Lo, and feel the weight of the Pulitzer in his hand....

"I have a right to be here," he whispered to the wiggling kitten. "This is *my* house. You can't just wake me up in the middle of the—"

A sound from downstairs interrupted him. Had a door creaked open?

Putting down the kitten, Max cocked his head. Nothing but silence. He frowned. He'd read all the articles in the shoe box—and found out plenty. Lo had never been married, though she'd dated a Meredith and Gersham V.P. From interviews, it was obvious that Sheldon Ferris felt betrayed and brokenhearted. But had Sheldon known Lo Lambert was pregnant?

Max heard another creak downstairs. Had Lo Lambert's supposed partner shown up here? *No. It's more likely she's had a falling-out with her accomplice—and he or she is the person from whom she needs protection....*

Or else *no one* was downstairs. The cottage was utterly silent now. Max just wished he was certain the baby was Sheldon's. Well, with any luck, Zach Forester would find out. Max had phoned Zach, and his P.I. friend had agreed to dig up all the dirt on Lo.

Max sat up straighter. A door *had* opened. Someone was definitely downstairs. If anything bad happened to Lo, it would be his fault, too. He never should have pretended to be her bodyguard. Chances were a criminal like her really needed one.

Rising cautiously, Max glanced around for a weapon. Nothing—unless he was going to defend the woman with boxes or books. He didn't even have a robe. Clad only in his boxers, he rubbed his stubbly jaw as he walked silently toward the door. He'd been sleeping like the dead. He always did, his first few nights home. And he felt too groggy to deal with intruders. Not that he had a choice.

He was halfway to Lo's room when sharp claws sank into the tender flesh of his ankle. He sighed. How was he supposed to defend Lo Lambert while her cat was attacking him? Dutifully lifting his foot, Max disengaged the kitten.

Then Max growled softly.

The terrified kitten peeped back, its two yellow eyes blinking in the dark. *Now, don't move,* Max thought, feeling faintly murderous. He glanced between Lo's closed door and the steps. What if *she* was downstairs? "Lo?" Max called. Realizing his mistake, he quickly added, "'Lo? Hello, down there. Is that you, Max?"

But no one answered.

And now the intruder knew Max was upstairs. *Great.* Max glanced at Lo's closed door again. If she awakened, he hoped she had enough common sense to stay put. Fortunately, the kitten was heading back to Max's room. Holding his breath, Max silently lowered himself to the first step, then the next and the next...

On the way down, his hand closed around a compact umbrella that had been shoved between the banister posts. It wasn't much of a weapon, but it would have to do. Max paused on the lowest step, as still as a statue. It was pitch-dark.

After a moment, he heard a rustle. Then soft, shallow breathing. Max craned his head toward the sounds. The other guy was crouched beneath the banister, next to a table not two feet from Max and the newel. Max could make out the faint silhouettes of a phone and lamp on the tabletop. Should he reach through the posts and flick on the lamp? It was the easiest way to get a look at the guy's face.

Yeah, and then he'll probably shoot me.

Or would he? Enough people were looking for Lo Lambert that the intruder could be anyone—even an overzealous lawman from the SEC or FBI. Max winced. Maybe he should have turned her in. Now he was guilty of harboring a fugitive. But no other reporter in the city would get an exclusive like this.

Or get to play house with a woman who looked like a goddess and kissed like a heaven-sent angel. Besides, when he'd felt her baby kick, it had taken away his breath. Surely he could seduce a confession out of her before he called the cops....

A loud creak sounded.

The guy realized Max was here—and was trying to escape! Max streaked around the newel with the speed of greased lightning. "Hold it right there," he snarled.

Just as Max lunged, a ghostly figure in a flowing white coat flew past. As the eerie apparition darted toward the living room, only its pounding footsteps assured Max it was human. He gave chase, clutching the umbrella and rounding the downstairs rooms, but the intruder was faster. Footsteps thudded full circle around the living room, kitchen and dining room.

On the third pass, Max pivoted and reversed directions, hoping to slam head-on into the guy. But the intruder did an about-face. Just as they reached the living room, Max flung out his umbrella-free hand and snatched at the intruder's filmy white coat-tails. The fabric whisked through Max's fingers, feeling strangely silken, then whipped around in the dark like a ghostly tail.

"Hey, Casper," Max muttered in a lethal tone. "I said stop."

Instead, the person darted upstairs. Max lunged again, this time catching a fistful of the coat. Simultaneously he pulled the intruder down onto the steps, tackled him and reached through the banister rails, jerking the lamp cord. Blinking against the brightness, Max could swear he'd just assaulted a bride.

Then she screamed bloody murder.

And Max realized he was lying flat on top of Lo Lambert. He groaned, thinking of the baby. "Oh, no, is it all right?"

"I am *not* an it," Lo said succinctly.

She was mad, Max realized. And even more annoying, she wasn't the least bit winded. How could a pregnant thief be in better shape than he was? "I mean the baby," he said flatly.

Lo sniffed haughtily. "Earlier you made it very clear what you think of my baby, so don't try to inquire about its health now."

Max's jaw set. "I like your baby just fine. It just surprised me." When her expression didn't soften in the least, he continued, "Clearly a little beauty sleep hasn't improved your mood."

"You think I need beauty sleep?"

Hardly. She was gorgeous. *And you need to get a story out of her,* Max reminded himself. He forced a smile. "Look, we seem to be getting off on the wrong foot..."

"I'm not sure I even still have a foot. You tackled me." She heaved an exaggerated sigh, then continued sweetly, "What? Were you having nightmares about some linebacker who creamed you back in high school?"

Max's temper flared. He wanted to remind her that she hardly deserved his protection since she belonged in jail. Feeling sorely tempted to call the precinct, he said, "Look, are you all right or not?"

"What do *you* think?"

She sounded fine. But he wasn't. Staring down, Max felt a traitorous tug of arousal in his nether regions. No wonder she'd looked like a ghost. She was wearing a sexy white nightie and a long, silky, pearl white robe, which was now hiked to her thighs. His tackle had landed her in an undeniably sensitive position—on her back with her knees parted. He was wedged between them, her bare skin teasing his upper thighs. All at once, he remembered he was clad only in boxers.

Color flooded her face as if she'd read his mind. Pressing her palms against his bare shoulders, she gave one hard shove. "What *is* your problem?"

He wouldn't know where to begin. First, she was a wanted criminal. And second, she'd caught him off guard and he was thoroughly aroused. "What's yours?"

"That should be obvious."

He started edging off her. She struggled to a half-sitting position, her outfit making her look incredibly innocent. Some men might like a woman in black—with those risqué garters and stockings with visible seams and black high heels that said, "Have your way with me."

Not Max.

Nothing excited him more than plain old white. He liked white blouses and cotton panties, too. The waist-high kind. His mouth went dry as he watched Lo tug down her hemline and quickly check her chest for exposed cleavage.

Catching his gaze, she snapped, "Would you please get off me?"

He lifted his eyes from her ample chest. "I *am* off you."

She scooted even farther away, the heat of their tussle still evident in the bright pink of her cheeks. "All the way off."

Max sighed. As he sat up, his thumb inadvertently pressed the trigger of the umbrella, and it popped open. For a minute he didn't move, merely held the umbrella over their heads as if they'd just been caught in a downpour.

And then Lo Lambert did the unforgivable. She started humming "Singing in the Rain."

"You're off-key," Max pointed out sourly.

Undeterred, she eyed the open umbrella. "Haven't you heard that's bad luck?"

Max thought of his redecorated cottage, the three-lettuce salad and the kitten. "Opening umbrellas indoors is the least of my troubles."

Lo giggled. "Were you really going to defend me with an umbrella?"

"Hardly." Max wrestled the umbrella shut. "But with you around, I knew to expect stormy weather. Besides, I left my gun at the...agency."

Her luscious green eyes widened. *Good.* Max stared back, gauging the reaction. Just exactly how much danger did Lo Lambert think she was in? And had she come downstairs to phone the accomplice who'd probably helped her set up all those price-fixing deals? If she had overseas accounts, she might have to check on them in the middle of the night because of the time difference.

"Don't worry." Max shoved the umbrella between the stair railing again. "I know you hired me for protection. I'll get a gun tomorrow." He glared pointedly at a wall clock. "Today."

Lo's gulp was audible. "I won't have a gun in my house."

Her house? That was rich. Nevertheless, Max felt relieved. Obviously, Lo didn't feel a gun was necessary. He eyed her suspiciously. "Mind telling me what you were doing down here?"

Her eyes slid guiltily away from his. "Oh, nothing."

She was lying. Maybe now, since she was in danger, she'd decided to leave town. No doubt she'd stashed the money she'd made backstabbing Meredith and Gersham clients in overseas accounts. "If you weren't doing anything, then why didn't you answer me?"

"I wanted to be alone."

Max rolled his eyes. "In the middle of the night? In the dark? Why—" He flashed her a quick smile. "I'm not sure you're entirely on the level."

Her voice rose indignantly. "Not on the level?"

He raised his hand. "Please," he said with exaggerated calm. "Not another hormonal episode."

Her jaw set stoically.

"If I'm going to protect you," he ground out, "I need to know what you're up to at all times."

"What I was doing is none of your business!"

Her eyes darted around so wildly that Max knew she was hiding something important. He could swear her lower lip had even trembled.

"C'mere, T-shirt," she said.

"T-shirt?" Max echoed just as the black-and-white kitten scampered down the steps, then hopped into Lo's arms. She nestled him against her shoulder, rubbing his fur against her cheek as if he were her last friend on earth. Intent on protecting his mistress, the kitten wrenched around and glared at Max.

Max almost smiled. The markings on the kitten did make it appear as if he were wearing a T-shirt. And he was kind of cute.... Max forced himself to look offended. "I thought you were—" *Sheldon Ferris or the FBI.* "A burglar."

Lo stared at him as if he were crazy. "Who would want to break in here?"

Max could think of countless people. "Someone. Otherwise you wouldn't need to hire a bodyguard, now, would you?"

Lo's face turned a guilty crimson, reminding Max that no matter how beautiful she was, she was trouble. His temper rose another notch. The woman might dress in virginal white, but she definitely had a black-lace soul. He became conscious that they were still sitting side by side on the steps, him in his underwear and her in her negligee.

Uncomfortable awareness sparked in her eyes, and Max realized she was steadfastly training her gaze above his waistline. He decided he'd better get moving. Abruptly, he stood. It hardly helped. Now he was towering over her. And staring down, he could see right between her breasts. Another traitorous tug of arousal threatened to pull him back on top of her again. He imagined himself kneeling down, raising her gown, sliding his palms up her silken thighs and...

"Would you please quit staring at me?" she said.

Max snapped back to reality. "Sorry," he said without thinking. "But you're easy to stare at."

Lo's expression softened, but only for an instant. "Just give it up, Boots. Nothing's going to happen between us."

Max sighed and stretched out his hand. "Here—"

Eyeing him warily, Lo readjusted T-shirt on her shoulder and gripped Max's hand. At the mere touch, tingles dusted his skin, and when he tugged, she headed right for his arms. Of course, she sidestepped at the last possible moment. As she skipped a few safe paces away, Max had to force himself not to reach out, grab her and simply demand the truth. *What are you doing down here?* he wanted to ask. *Why were you so desperate to hide from me?*

And then he heard a loud ding.

He glanced in the direction of the kitchen. Lo had

apparently installed a doorbell for the back door. No doubt she'd been expecting someone—and possibly a dangerous someone. Max peered into her nervous eyes, then he swiftly pivoted and headed for the kitchen.

Pure panic was in her voice. "Wait!"

From behind, she grabbed his biceps and Max looked at her over his shoulder. His voice turned testy. "What's in that kitchen you don't want me to see?"

"Please," she begged. "Just go upstairs."

It would take far more than Lo Lambert's wheedling to stop him. Max strode toward the kitchen again. Inside, he quickly flicked on the light—and nearly choked. No wonder she'd begged him not to look.

His horrified eyes trailed over the counters and tabletop—over cans and jars, past an open pint of ice cream and a half-eaten bag of barbecued potato chips. Finally, his gaze rested on her plate. It was heaped with steaming leftover turkey, dressing and gravy. Smack-dab in the middle of the mess was a huge dollop of melting green, mint-chocolate-chip ice cream.

Another ding sounded.

It wasn't a doorbell, Max realized now. It was a microwave oven. He turned very slowly toward the glass door—and found himself staring at a baked potato.

Somehow, Max forced himself to keep turning—and face Lo Lambert. She looked positively mortified. Her eyes searched his, gauging his reaction to her gluttonous food binge. His mind raced, searching for something to say, but Lo Lambert had a way of rendering him speechless.

"I—I'm not usually—usually like this," she said haltingly. "It—it's just since the pregnancy…" T-shirt squirmed on her chest, and Lo quickly placed him on the floor as if relieved to focus on anything other than Max.

Max recalled her untouched dinner plate—and his chest squeezed tight. He couldn't afford to like the woman, since she was the object of his journalistic investigation, but she was sure making it difficult. He'd been so convinced she was up to no good. But she'd merely been hungry. And she was eating for two.

Lo suddenly looked from the kitten to Max's eyes. "Uh…he was a stray," she explained.

There was a long silence. Her cheeks turned bright red. Not from guilt, Max now knew, but embarrassment. "You know," Max managed to say. "I could sure use that piece of pie you promised me for dessert."

Her audible sigh of relief made him wince. "Uh—" She swallowed hard. "Why don't you just sit down and let me get it for you?"

Max seated himself at the table. A second later, Lo served him not one, but two slices of pie—both pumpkin and pecan. When she grabbed the ice-cream scoop and reached for the green ice cream, now forming puddles in the pint container, Max raised his hand. "Really," he assured her, "this is plenty for me."

She gulped. "Sorry."

Max nodded at her colorful plate. "Please…"

"I am a little hungry," she said.

Now that's an understatement. He watched her scoot sideways into her chair, a hand resting on her belly. Against his will, his eyes drifted over her thick red hair. It was sexily disheveled and layered mussily around her face. Her green eyes sparkled like emeralds and her kissable pink mouth was pouty. Max was sure he'd never seen a woman quite so pretty. He forced himself to look away, only to find himself staring into the disgusting swirl of green mint ice cream melting into her turkey gravy. When Lo caught him looking, he smiled with encouragement.

"Dig in," he suggested.

She shot him such a relieved, grateful glance that he could have just rescued a small child from a burning building. Then as she lifted her spoon and savored a heaping mouthful of the ice-cream-and-gravy mixture, she looked up and smiled a smile that warmed him to his very soul.

Break my heart, Max thought. Whatever Lo Lambert had done, she was making him feel things he hadn't for years. Maybe not since Molly Miller, back in grade school.

"Good?" he inquired as she took another bite.

Lo was chewing, so she merely shut her eyes and moaned softly. Finally, she licked a fleck of chocolate chip from her upper lip. Then, in a breathy, reverent voice, she whispered, "Pure heaven."

So's looking at you, honey, Max thought.

And that's when he knew that turning her in wasn't exactly going to be easy.

6

If At First You Don't Succeed...

MAX'S PRIZE CORVETTE sputtered and coughed, then suddenly lunged like a bright red panther into Colleen's driveway. Even in the darkness, Max could see that Lo's bad driving skills were making her blush. As well they should. He clenched his teeth as his sorely misused car shuddered to a halt. "Who the hell taught you to drive a standard?" he couldn't help but growl.

"Uh...I'm self-taught."

Obviously. And, no doubt, Lo had taught herself by driving *his* standard.

Before Max could say anything further, Lo quickly continued, "I just can't believe Colleen sent us to the 7-Eleven for drinks *again*."

Max could. Ever since their arrival at the July fourth block party, all Lo's matchmaking neighbors had made sure Max and Lo stayed joined at the hip. Apparently they thought he was an old friend of hers and a potential "catch." Melvin Rhys had even gone so far as to jokingly introduce Max around as "Maxine's latest lover."

Max only wished. Especially when he glanced over Lo's outfit—a floral print sundress and a wide-brimmed straw hat. "Hot to Trot" pink toenails peeked from her bright blue sandals. She looked so sexy it made up for the fact that she'd destroyed the clutch on his Corvette. Well, almost.

"She did just tell us to get more soft drinks, right?"

Max nodded, deciding the neighbors probably thought he was an old friend of Lo's. "Yeah." As he reached behind his seat for the drinks, Max glanced through the back windshield—and suddenly froze. If he'd been seriously thinking about turning Lo in to the cops, now was definitely the time.

A man in uniform was headed right for them.

Apparently, the cop had been about to hop inside his police cruiser when he'd spotted them. Now he was weaving around the countless vehicles double-parked near Colleen's. Max took quick inventory. Was a taillight broken on the Corvette? Was the sticker outdated? The license plate missing?

But no...

The ruined clutch aside, Max's car was in perfect shape. So what did the cop want? And would he recognize Lo? Maybe not. Her pictures in the papers were of such poor quality that even Dotty Jansen hadn't recognized her—at least not yet.

Lo, still oblivious to the cop, tapped her "Hot to Trot" fingernails on the steering wheel. "C'mon, Boots. In a car this size, I seriously doubt you've lost those sodas."

"They're right here," Max murmured.

And so was the cop. Visions of a high-speed car pursuit flashed through Max's mind. Should he tell Lo to punch the gas and make a run for it? If he did, he'd blow his own cover, and Lo would know Max knew who she really was....

Goodbye Pulitzer, Max thought.

He eyed the cop, who was three car lengths away...now two. Suddenly, Max sat up straight. He had to act—and fast. Lo was staring warily at him, her eyes narrowed.

"Is something wrong?"

"Look," Max said abruptly, "all week long, I've kept my hands off you. And...well, sorry, but I just can't do it anymore."

Lo gaped at him.

And while her mouth was still like that—hanging wide open—Max smacked his lips down on hers and simply kissed her good and hard. Somehow, he didn't expect her to kiss him back. But she did. And when her arms circled his neck in the cramped confines of the car, and her delicate, velvet lips nibbled his, Max forgot all about the cop...

Until the cop cleared his throat.

Wrenched back to the present, Max jerked up his head—and found himself looking into a pair of suspicious dark eyes. The man had brown curly hair and a brass nameplate on his blue uniform pocket that said Sergeant Mack.

"Ahem." Sergeant Mack had the decency to look embarrassed. "So sorry to interrupt."

Max swiftly leaned across Lo's lap, thrusting his head through her window, hoping to obscure her from view. He mustered his friendliest, most trustworthy chuckle. "You're not nearly as sorry as I am, Officer. But what can I do for you?"

Sergeant Mack leaned down, forcing Max to retreat inside the car. He held his breath as the cop rested his elbows on Lo's window frame. Fortunately, her floppy hat brim was hiding her face. Besides, the top was up on the convertible, making the car's interior even darker than outside. If the police had better pictures of Lo than what had run in the papers, Sergeant Mack still might not recognize her....

As the officer's eyes pierced the car's interior, he shoved a black-and-white picture of Lo through the open window. "I'm looking for a woman named Lo Lambert. You've probably read about her in the papers. Have either of you seen her?"

Lo made a small choking sound.

Max peered hard at the picture. No doubt the officer had just shown it around the block party. Fortunately, people were preoccupied with having a good time. Maybe no one stopped to carry the photo to a light and scrutinize it. Still, even though the photo was bad, Max couldn't believe no one recognized her.

"Have you seen her?" Sergeant Mack repeated.

Max shook his head. "Can't say as I have."

"No," Lo squeaked.

"Was that a no, ma'am?"

The wide brim of Lo's hat flopped up and down. "Yes. I mean, no. I mean, yes, that was a no."

Max leaned across her lap again. "What she means is that we've never seen that woman."

"We would have reported it first thing!" Lo exclaimed nervously.

Sergeant Mack stared down at her hat brim for a long moment. Max became aware of the hard, heavy beat of his own heart, and of the dull dread that had settled in the pit of his stomach. As he waited for Sergeant Mack to yank Lo from the car and arrest her, Max slipped his arm around her, dangling his hand in such a way that it would better obscure her face.

Suddenly, Sergeant Mack winked. "Well, I guess I'll let you two get back to your—er—business. Like I say, I'm truly sorry to interrupt, but this woman's a fugitive. Not that you two should worry. Both New York and Connecticut police are doing everything possible to apprehend her." His smile broadened. "And if at first we don't succeed..."

"You just try, try again?" Lo supplied weakly.

"That's right, ma'am."

Lo's voice quavered. "That makes me feel so relieved."

Max gave Lo's thigh a soothing pat, then nodded manfully at Sergeant Mack. "We have total faith in the police."

Only when Sergeant Mack backed away did Max duck his head and glimpse under Lo's hat brim. From the O of her glistening, lip-glossed mouth, he could tell she was blowing out a long, silent breath.

"Well, I hope they find that woman," Max forced himself to say. To his relief, his voice sounded convincing. Lo would never guess he knew who she was.

"It's frightening to think of a criminal like that running loose," Lo said shakily.

Max wanted to end the strained conversation, but it seemed the perfect opportunity to pump her for information. "So you've read about Lo Lambert in the papers?"

With her thumbnail, Lo worried a nonexistent speck on the steering wheel. "Not much. Mostly I just read the papers to check the weather."

Feeling disappointed, Max nodded as if he never read newspapers, either. Then he grabbed the sodas. By the time he got out, circled the car and opened the door for Lo, Colleen was waving at them from the yard.

"We're about ready to start the fireworks!" she shouted.

Max put his palm on the small of Lo's back and guided her toward a group of lawn chairs in the yard, only stopping to leave the sodas on a picnic table. When they reached the chairs, he half expected someone to point at Lo and scream, "That's Lo Lambert!" Instead, Melvin Rhys's hairy hand clamped down on Max's shoulder. As soon as the suburban gorilla had made sure Max was seated next to Lo, he whirled around in his own lawn chair and glared at his sons.

"Timmy," Melvin roared. "Quit chasing Jeffie with that baseball bat."

"And you girls—" Colleen shouted from somewhere. "Keep your bikes out of Mr. Dickerson's flower beds."

Lo suddenly leaned forward in her chair and laughed, making Max wonder how she could remain so cool under pressure. Was that a further indication of her guilt?

"You think Howie managed to organize his contest while we were gone?" Lo asked.

Even though Max was still eyeing the cop cruiser in the driveway, he managed a chuckle. When they'd left for the 7-Eleven, seven-year-old Howie was trying to organize a hot-dog-eating contest. The runner-up was the first person who could make him or herself throw up. First place went to whoever threw up the most. "Even if he did," Max said, "I wasn't going to enter."

Lo shot Max a disdainful glance. "Afraid I'd win?"

Max's lips twitched. "Pregnancy might give you an edge."

Their eyes met. For a second, the sights and sounds of the block party seemed to recede—the scents of charcoal and burnt burgers, the kids wearing more mustard and ketchup than they'd eaten, and the teenage girls self-consciously tossing their hair while strutting boys pretended to ignore them.

And then the quick whoop of a siren sounded. Lo started as if someone had lit a fire beneath her. Max turned and stared at the driveway again, watching as Sergeant Mack snapped on his headlights. The cruiser glided down the street, then turned a corner and vanished.

Max hardly felt relieved. It was only a matter of time until the woman next to him was found and hauled off to jail. Max was still staring thoughtfully at the empty roadway where the car had been, when he heard Lo's voice. "Did you just say something, Helen?"

Max glanced at the two elderly spinsters who'd just seated themselves across from him and Lo. Both

Helen and Gladys had been mere weeks from retirement when the Dreamy Diapers plant shut down.

Now Helen tapped her hearing aid, raising her voice to a near shout. Max wished she hadn't. Because she screamed, "I *said* I think it's just *lovely* that you and Boots are *lovers!*"

Lo plastered a smile on her face. Under her breath, she whispered, "I can't believe Melvin told her that. Not that she really believes it," Lo added quickly. "Everybody knows I'm not that kind of girl."

Max gave her a suggestive once-over. "At least not yet."

Helen hadn't heard the exchange. She dragged a hand through her blue-rinsed hair. "Well, you know what Gladys just *happened* to say to me the other day?" she said brightly to Max.

Max shot her a teasing smile. "I'm afraid to ask."

Helen clasped her hands more tightly in her lap. "Well, Gladdy said that pregnant women *always* make the best wives. Now, didn't you say *exactly* that to me, Gladdy?"

Gladys looked thoroughly confused. Then she exclaimed, "Why, of course I did! I really did! Why, I most *certainly* did!"

"Enough matchmaking," Lo said flatly.

Max laughed. Then he draped his arm around Lo, cupping her bare shoulder with his palm. He just wished things weren't getting so complicated. It felt so good to be here with Lo and the neighbors. All week, he'd caught himself thinking about how he'd always put his career before relationships and that he'd never met the right woman. And then, suddenly, almost magically, he'd found Lo Lambert cooking in his kitchen....

Timmy Rhys's sudden scream broke into Max's reverie. "Look out!"

Max's head veered up. The next thing he knew he was on his feet—catching Timmy Rhys's baseball barehanded. The tightly packed white leather ball stung every nerve in Max's hand, even after he set it aside.

"No more baseball for you, tonight!" Melvin Rhys shouted. "You could have broken a window."

"Or my hand," Max muttered with mock grumpiness.

Lo chuckled and made a show of checking his palm for broken bones. "You'll live." She shot him a quick grin. "And it *was* a great catch."

Helen was clapping her hands in delight. "Did you see that, Gladdy?"

Gladys nodded. "My, oh, my. He caught that ball barehanded."

Helen pulled her shawl around her shoulders and nodded approvingly. "I told you he'd make a fine father."

"He most certainly would," replied Gladys.

Lo laughed nervously, her face turning crimson. She leaned forward, grabbing a blanket at her feet. "C'mon, Boots. Let's get ready for the fireworks."

Max caught her hand and stood. As he pulled her close, he chuckled. "Honey," he teased, "you *are* the fireworks."

"Leaving us?" Helen inquired.

Lo nodded. "We figured we'd find a spot on the grass."

Gladys and Helen exchanged a pointed look, as if to say watching fireworks was the last thing Max and Lo would be doing. Against his will, Max felt a smile steal over his lips. "Is that all right with you two?"

Gladys and Helen giggled. "Don't do anything I wouldn't do," Helen tittered.

Within moments, Max had laid the blanket on the grass and sprawled next to Lo. "Perfect," he said, sighing. It was completely dark, and all around them the kids were falling quiet, waiting for the fireworks. Max just wished the evening hadn't been marred by the intrusion of Sergeant Mack. Realizing the police were canvassing the neighborhood for Lo was a definite reality check.

Max's eyes drifted over her. She was lying on her back, her belly large, her face clear and beautiful. She clasped her hands beneath her breasts. Up on his elbow, Max gazed down. And suddenly frowned. Earlier in the week, he'd heard the phone ring, but later, Lo had sworn there had been no call.

"I heard the phone," Max had said. "Was it him?"

Lo had flushed. "Who?"

"Him." Max had wanted to say her ex-husband, but he knew she'd never really been married. "Whoever's bothering you."

Finally, pure worry crossed Lo's features. She'd nodded and started wringing her hands. "It *was* him. Oh, I just know everything's going to turn out badly."

Unexpected protective feelings had welled within Max. Not that he could help her hide forever. Zach Forester had called that same day. The P.I. told Lo he was from the agency, as Max had instructed him, and so she'd cautiously handed over the phone. According to Zach, there were mountains of hard evidence against her—phone records and computer disks. Whenever she turned up, Zach said, Lo Lambert was going where the sun didn't shine.

If whoever's bothering her doesn't harm her first, Max thought now.

"Look, er, Maxine," Max suddenly said. "You left the house without me a couple times this week." She'd sneaked out before he'd realized she was gone, and each time, he'd been convinced she was meeting her accomplice. But then she'd returned with a quart of milk or an ice-cream bar.

Lo raised her eyebrows. "So?"

"So, I'm your bodyguard." It wasn't exactly true, but then Max *had* just rescued her from the cops. "And I don't want you leaving the house alone again."

"I only went out to get milk this morning," Lo scoffed. "The 7-Eleven's right around the corner."

"Promise," Max said simply.

He felt her eyes drifting over him—from his finger-combed hair to his face, then down to the open neck of his tight, short-sleeved shirt. Her eyes followed the shirt's pearl snaps, stopped at his belt buckle, then shot to his eyes again.

"Okay. You can come everywhere with me. I promise." She flashed him a quick smile. "Satisfied?"

Max grinned. "Everywhere?"

She smirked, well aware he was thinking of her bed. "*Almost* everywhere."

"Not entirely satisfying, but it'll do."

"It'll have to."

Max shot her a smile that said, "For now." Then his eyes traveled back toward the central action of the block party. He'd seen Lo interact with so many people today—the Rhyses, Helen and Gladys and Colleen.... Max's chest constricted. No matter what happened, the truth was going to come to light. Lo would lose her hard-won status in the community, and there was no way he could protect her. His eyes swept the length of her—all the way down her long, luscious legs to her feet.

"I swear," he murmured. "You've got the sexiest feet I've ever seen."

She wiggled her toes.

Somehow, Max refrained from saying that her feet would be even sexier if they knew how to work his clutch. Fortunately, Lo's gaze didn't register the sudden heat that flushed his skin as he looked at her—or the sharp, undeniable tug of arousal that made him take a deep breath. Staring intensely into her eyes, he resolved to get to the bottom of whatever had happened. Tomorrow, he'd ask for the day off. Lo had plans to shop for baby clothes with Dotty, which meant she'd be safe. Meantime, Max would quit playing bodyguard and start playing detective.

As the first fireworks lit up the sky, Max tangled his fingers through Lo's hair, catching the silken strands in fistfuls. When she didn't protest, he kissed her gently.

"What did you do that for?" she murmured.

He could think of a thousand reasons. Finally, he

PLAY "LUCKY 7" AND GET
FIVE FREE GIFTS!

HOW TO PLAY:

1. With a coin, carefully scratch off the silver box at the right. Then check the claim ch⋯ to see what we have for you—**FREE BOOKS** and a gift—**ALL YOURS! ALL FREE!**

2. Send back this card and you'll receive brand-new Harlequin Love & Laughter™ nove⋯ These books have a cover price of $3.99 each, but they are yours to keep absolutely fre⋯

3. There's no catch. You're under no obligation to buy anything. We charge nothing— ZERO—for your first shipme⋯ And you don't have to mak⋯ any minimum number of purchases—not even one!

4. The fact is thousands of readers enjoy receiving books by mail from the Harlequin Reader Service® months before they're available in stores. They like the convenience ⋯ home delivery and they love our discount prices!

5. We hope that after receiving your free books you'll want to remain a subscriber. But the choice is yours—to continue or cancel, any time at all! So why not take us up on ⋯ invitation, with no risk of any kind. You'll be glad you did!

YOURS FREE!

You'll love this exquisite necklace, set with an elegant simulated pearl pendant! It's the perfect accessory to dress up any outfit, casual or formal — and is yours ABSOLUTELY FREE when you accept our NO-RISK offer!

NOT ACTUAL SIZE

NO COST! NO OBLIGATION TO BUY!
NO PURCHASE NECESSARY!

PLAY THE

LUCKY 7
SLOT MACHINE GAME!

Just scratch off the silver box with a coin. Then check below to see the gifts you get!

YES!

I have scratched off the silver box. Please send me all the gifts for which I qualify. I understand I am under no obligation to purchase any books, as explained on the back and on the opposite page.

302 CIH CARG
(C-H-LL-07/97)

Name

Address   Apt.#

City   Prov.   Postal Code

7	7	7	**WORTH FOUR FREE BOOKS PLUS A FREE HEART PENDANT!**
cherries	cherries	cherries	**WORTH THREE FREE BOOKS!**
clover	clover	clover	**WORTH TWO FREE BOOKS!**
bell	bell	cherries	**WORTH ONE FREE BOOK!**

Offer limited to one per household and not valid to current Harlequin Love & Laughter™ subscribers. All orders subject to approval.

The Harlequin Reader Service® —Here's how it works

If offer card is missing, write to: Harlequin Reader Service, P.O. Box 609, Fort Erie, Ontario L2A 5X3

0195619199-L2A5X3-BR01

HARLEQUIN READER SERVICE
PO BOX 609
FORT ERIE ON   L2A 9Z9

Canada Post Corporation/Société canadienne des postes

Postage paid   Port payé
If mailed in Canada   si posté au Canada

Business   Réponse
Reply   d'affaires

0195619199   01

MAIL ▶ POSTE

nodded up at the fireworks bursting in the sky. "Because that's how you make me feel."

"How's that?"

Max's chuckle was barely audible. "Like I'm about to explode."

"I don't intend to pursue this," she warned.

"And," he said before his lips found hers again, "I don't intend to stop."

ZACH FORESTER'S PLACE WAS in a Wall Street high-rise and had more security than the White House—a curb man, a doorman, a deskman staring at a bank of monitors, cameras in the halls and elevators, an intercom outside the apartment door.

Max put his face right in front of Zach's peephole. "I swear it's really me, Zach."

The intercom sounded. "Do you have your press credentials?"

Max sighed and picked up the phone next to the door. "Yes, but don't you think you're getting a little paranoid?"

"Years of doing surveillance work does this to a guy."

Max sighed and dutifully held his *New York Times* card against the peephole.

One by one, locks began to turn over. They didn't stop until Max counted seven. When the door swung open and Zach wasn't in sight, Max was almost afraid to go inside.

Then Zach stepped from behind the door. The P.I., who was in his early thirties, had longish brown hair pulled into a tight queue and bright blue eyes that popped out of his gaunt, wizened face. He was wear-

ing black Lycra cycling pants and a black T-shirt that
said Who Needs Friends When You Have A Computer?

Max shook his head. "I think you've been on the
Internet too long."

Zach's sudden, hearty laugh reverberated in the
cavernous apartment. "Probably. C'mon in."

The interior was relatively normal, although the
high-ceilinged space was open and airy, presumably
so Zach would quickly notice any intruders unfortunate enough to invade his home. In one corner, an
island shaped the kitchen space. In another, steps led
to an elevated hot tub and bath.

"Follow me," Zach instructed. "And I'll show
you everything I've got on Lo Lambert."

His tone didn't sound promising. Max followed,
seating himself in a director's chair, then he glanced
at Zach's workstation—a simple polished oak desk,
a high-end computer system and file cabinets that had
seen better days.

Zach handed him a file. "Everything's there. I
tapped into Meredith and Gersham's files and downloaded some of the stuff."

Max stared at Zach. "Legal?"

Zach smirked. "Do you want my methods or results?"

Max sighed. "Results."

"Then don't ask."

Max stared down at the file again, then riffled
through the papers. Most were rows of numerical figures. Legal briefs for deals that were suspect.
Minutes from meetings.

"Basically," Zach said, "the SEC is ready to arrest a number of executives, but they're holding off until they find Lo Lambert. If they can't break her down and make her confess, then they'll cut deals with the other guys, who'll probably turn her in.''

Max glanced over the papers dealing with the Dreamy Diapers packaging plant in his neighborhood. ''They have hard evidence on the owner of the Dreamy plant?''

Zach nodded. ''Sure. And on a guy who runs a pharmaceutical company, as well as others. But like I say, they won't make arrests until they find Lo Lambert. She's the link to all of the illegal deals.''

Max stared down. It was all here in black and white. One memo, signed by Lo, overtly set up a price-fixing deal between two other parties. He shoved the paper to the back of the file, thinking he'd read through the materials more carefully later. Then he realized Zach was staring at him. ''What?''

''Just let me get this straight,'' Zach said. ''Lo Lambert is living in your house and using your name. And she thinks you're a bodyguard she hired from some agency?''

Max nodded. ''Yeah, this is supposed to be my day off. I'm catching a plane in a couple of hours. I'm going to see her grandmother. Did anybody question her?''

Zach shook his head. ''No, she's in a nursing home.''

''That doesn't mean she can't talk.''

Zach stared at him a long time, then groaned. ''I knew it. You're attracted to Lo Lambert, and now you're starting to think she might be innocent.''

Max shrugged. ''Maybe.''

"Well—" Zach nodded at the file in Max's hand "—she's not. And if you want to see what becomes of the men that woman chews up and spits out, I suggest you go see Sheldon Ferris."

FERRIS'S OFFICE WAS impressive. His massive, black-lacquered desk was positioned on a raised platform, and behind it, floor-to-ceiling windows offered a stunning view of Manhattan's skyline. The place looked more like a movie set than the kind of office a man worked in, so Max glanced around, expecting to find an office behind the office. Instead, he saw Sheldon Ferris breeze into the room.

"So sorry to keep you waiting!"

Max stood. Sheldon's handshake was firm, his stride confident, and the man was impeccably groomed. His nails were as buffed as his shoes and his hair had probably been barbered that morning. While he seemed perfectly likable, Max bristled. All his journalistic feelers started to wiggle. Or was that just jealousy? Probably, he thought. After all, Max couldn't bear to think of this man with Lo. Max's eyes narrowed as Sheldon stepped onto the raised platform, circled his desk and took the seat behind it.

"Please, have a seat," Sheldon said.

When Max sat, he realized he had no choice but to stare up at Sheldon. *It's like the guy thinks he's a god, perched on a mighty tower,* Max thought. Then he felt a rush of anger at himself. This interview was work, not personal. *Don't let your jealousy get in the way of your objectivity.* "Mr. Ferris, thanks for seeing me on such short notice."

"I've only got a second, but I'm glad to make time for a member of the press. Especially someone as important as yourself." Sheldon flashed Max a smile. "I do read—and enjoy—your column."

The man was definitely too ingratiating. But then, that could be Max's jealousy talking again. "What can you tell me about your relationship with Lo Lambert?"

Sheldon leaned forward and stared into Max's eyes, as if deciding whether or not to trust him. Then he gushed, "Oh, this whole ordeal has been awful."

"Awful?"

"I still love her. I want her back. I want her found. I—" Sheldon's voice broke. "I don't know what to do anymore, where to turn…"

Max clenched his teeth. In a mental flash, he imagined Sheldon and Lo being reunited in a prison visiting area. They were sitting on opposite sides of a glass wall, gazing lovingly at each other and murmuring pillow talk into their individual phone receivers. Forcing his attention back to the matter at hand, Max said, "Mr. Ferris, did you have any inkling that Lo Lambert was fixing prices behind your back?"

Sheldon straightened his tie nervously. "No. Not at all."

If he was lying, Max thought, he sure was good. "I got an anonymous tip…" Max let his voice trail off, wondering if Sheldon would get nervous.

He didn't. He raised his eyebrows innocently. His voice was hopeful. "About Lo?"

Max nodded. "An anonymous tip that she was pregnant with your child when the scandal broke."

Sheldon's only reaction was to exhale a deep sigh. "It's possible. But I don't know." Suddenly, he buried his face in his hands. "I can't bear to think of my own child being cared for by a women who—who—" His voice cracked. "Broke so many laws. Who betrayed me like this."

"I'm really very sorry," Max intoned dutifully.

"No, *I'm* sorry." Tears shimmered in Sheldon's eyes. "I thought I could do this interview, but I can't. I've already told everything to the police. I hope you'll understand that talking about her upsets me."

Max rose and slid his card across Sheldon's desk. "That's my number at the *Times*. Feel free to call me. Even if I'm not there, I regularly check my voice mail."

As Max turned to go, he felt pure disappointment. Either Sheldon Ferris had really lost his heart to a criminal. Or he was the most practiced liar Max had ever met.

7

When Falling in Love, Expect the Unexpected

"YOU SAY YOU FLEW in from Connecticut to talk to me about marrying my granddaughter?"

Max hadn't said that at all. "Uh, Mrs. Lambert, that's not—"

"Just call me Gran—" Gran's booming voice was at complete odds with her small body and wiry movements, "—seeing as we're family now."

"But, Mrs. Lam—er—*Gran*—" Max cut himself off, thinking that Josephine Lambert was the most impossible person he'd ever met.

She was propped up in an overstuffed armchair, her hands angelically folded in her lap and a crucifix mounted on the wall behind her. She had Lo's lush mouth and green eyes, hair that was dyed more orange than auburn, and new white Reeboks that peeked from the longish velour pants of her bright blue running suit. Only her sun-browned skin, which was as wrinkled as a prune's, served as a confession that she was closer to eighty than seventy.

"Well—" A smiling, thirtyish blonde whose name tag read Cassie lingered hesitantly by the door. "I guess I can just leave you two alone..."

At first, Max thought the attendant was worried

about leaving Gran with a strange man. Then he realized Cassie was trying to protect *him*. He watched in amazement as Gran fixed the woman with the meanest, evilest stare he'd ever seen.

"Before you go," Gran said, "could you do me just one *measly* favor?"

Cassie gulped. "What?"

"Promise me you'll never come back!"

Cassie glanced helplessly at Max. "Please, Mrs. Lambert, we're doing our very best to accommodate you here—"

Gran swiveled toward Max. "See how she treats me! Isn't this place awful?" Her green eyes narrowed. "I'm sure they sent my poor, gullible granddaughter a fake brochure! The Fountain of Youth nursing home—ha! Why, if Lo had actually visited this place, she'd never have signed me on! And now that I told her how horrible it is, she's going to move me to Connecticut as soon as possible!"

"But we *do* want you to be happy," Cassie ventured.

"Mother Teresa could not find happiness here!"

Max rolled his eyes. Right. Ivana Trump would have been ecstatic. The place was costing Max a fortune. Josephine occupied her own well-appointed apartment—although lately she'd become such a handful that the staff was threatening to move her to an assisted living area. On the hour, minivans were at her disposal—heading to town, a bowling alley and local movie theaters. Other amenities included an on-the-premises chapel that offered daily mass, a garden, swimming pool and hair salon. Regular manicures and pedicures were given door-to-door.

"This isn't a nursing home," Max muttered. "This is a resort."

"I heard that, young man," Gran said as Cassie left. "Just because I'm old, don't you dare make the mistake of thinking I'm deaf."

"You may not be deaf," Max shot back, "but you sure have selective hearing."

At that, respect actually shone in Gran's eyes. Max was glad, too. He wasn't about to let her railroad him the way she did the staff. He didn't care how old she was.

"Well...I can see why you'd want to marry Lo," she remarked.

So, it's back to that theme again. Max coldly assessed her. He was sure she'd heard him right the first time, but he supposed there was a slight chance her hearing aids really weren't working. "I said I came to *talk* about your granddaughter, not to talk about marrying her."

"Marrying her?" Gran echoed innocently. "Why, pardon me for mentioning it, young man, but didn't you already say you were marrying her?"

"No, I—"

Gran abruptly cut off Max by heading toward the Lo Lambert picture shrine on top of the TV. "Well," she said, moving a Madonna figurine aside with real reverence, "I guess you must have dropped by to see all of Lo's baby pictures."

"Dropped by? I said I *flew* down—"

"You're down with the flu? Why, that can be just terrible in summer!"

Max sighed. "Look, Mrs. Lam—"

"Gran," she corrected.

"Look, *Gran,* I didn't come to see baby pic—"

"Well, not to worry. We'll start with grade school." Gran pointed at a silver-framed photograph next to the TV remote. "This is your future wife on her very first day of school. And here she is in drama club and pep club and..."

Every possible club known to man, Max thought. Suddenly, he leaned forward. "And she was a majorette?"

"Well, she *would* have been homecoming queen, too, but during games she had to twirl." Gran sighed as she crossed the room again, this time dropping a heavy photo album in Max's lap. "I always said that was the real pity about her otherwise pristine educational career."

Max opened the photo album. "What was?"

Gran shook her head sadly. "That my poor Lo just couldn't clone herself."

Somehow, Max refrained from saying that if Lo Lambert had cloned herself, she would have wreaked twice as much havoc at Meredith and Gersham. As he turned the pages of the album, he began to frown. Lo had been such a smiling baby. An adorable toddler.

Gran pointed down, her voice softening. "And that was my son."

In the picture, Lo's father was young and strong and handsome. The pretty woman beside him possessed Lo's lush curves and smile. A baby that must have been Lo was in her arms. They all looked so happy.... Max turned page after page, not sure what he was looking for. He'd booked the flight here just hoping to find...*something.*

Now, Max wasn't sure which he found more disconcerting—that he was so attracted to such a seeming Goody Two-shoes, or that he couldn't reconcile Lo the majorette with Lo the criminal mastermind. Thinking of Sheldon Ferris's heartbroken expression, Max wondered if Zach was right. Did Lo really chew men up and spit them out?

Max had become so engrossed in the album that when he finally raised his gaze to a wall clock, he started. If he didn't hurry, he'd miss his return plane. Glancing in Gran's general direction, he found himself staring inside an emptied closet. Coat hangers still swung on the bar. Even worse, a huge suitcase was on the floor into which Gran was quickly stuffing all her clothes.

Max stared at her warily. "What are you doing?"

"What do you think?"

"Packing?" Max ventured.

"Obviously. And if you keep making moronic observations like that, young man, I might decide you're nowhere near smart enough for my granddaughter. She's brilliant, you know." Gran whirled toward him. "You *did* say you'd come to take me to Connecticut, didn't you?"

"I said no such thing." If Lo *had* robbed Meredith and Gersham clients—something Max was starting desperately to hope wasn't true—he at least now knew where she'd gotten the genes for devious behavior. *But it is true, Max. Zach's given you ample evidence....* He realized Gran was glaring at him.

"If you really intend to leave me in this horrible dungeon for the aged," Gran burst out, "then you might as well just go ahead and call in Dr. Kevorkian!''

Max groaned. "Please, you have to understand..."

"My granddaughter *is* in Connecticut, isn't she?" Terror crossed Gran's features. "Or have you done something with her?"

Now she was trying to make Max sound like an ax murderer. "Hardly," he said.

"Then there should be no problem with taking me to her!"

Max merely sighed and watched for long, stunned moments as Gran continued packing. Her back was ramrod straight, her chin defiant. The lady was going to Connecticut, come hell or high water. He cringed when she smoothed her little blue running suit, jumped agilely onto her suitcase and zipped it.

Then she stood. "Now, I'll just get my pocketbook."

"I'm not leaving you in a dungeon," Max said flatly. "I'm leaving you *here*, in this tastefully decorated apartment."

"You're not leaving me anywhere," Gran corrected. "And you'd better prepare to carry my suitcase, young man. Because I'm old and it's heavy."

Clutching her purse, Gran stopped right in front of him. Maybe she'd always been short. Or else she'd shrunk with age. Either way, she had to crane her neck at an impossible angle to glare at him. She looked feisty and yet fragile. Brittle as a cracker, but sharp as a tack.

"I *can't*," Max said. Then he tried his best to ignore her trembling lower lip and the two fat tears that welled in her green, Lo-like eyes. *Damn*. She was supposed to be a fighter, not a crier.

"Please," she whispered.

How could this little old lady be getting the best of him? "I said no," Max whispered back.

"But I hate minivan rides," she grumbled miserably. "And shopping malls and manicures and bowling."

Max shrugged helplessly. "What *would* make you happy?"

Gran sniffled. "If you would let me see my Lo."

"Aw, hell," Max muttered. And then he said, "Please, Mrs. Lam—er, Gran. Don't worry. I can't take you today, but I swear I'll be back."

"OH, NO..." LO MURMURED. As she wedged the phone receiver beneath her chin, one of the straps of her delicate, mint green sundress fell off a sun pink shoulder.

"Is it *him?*" Max mouthed.

Lo hooked a thumb under the recalcitrant shoulder strap and slid it back into place. "No," she mouthed back.

The possessive way she was clutching the phone made Max feel downright righteous, as if he really were her bodyguard and had every right to monitor her private conversations.

Well, as long as the caller wasn't threatening her, Max didn't care who it was. At least that's what he told himself. Feigning indifference, he fanned himself against the heat in the kitchen, then ran a flattened palm over his head, slicking back his hair. A second later, he untucked his denim shirt from his threadbare jeans and tugged on a shirttail, undoing all the snaps.

There. He was cooler. And Lo had noticed his bare chest. *Okay, so maybe I'm posing for her,* he thought. Leaning back to get a better look at her, he looped a thumb through his front belt loop so his fingers grazed the oval silver buckle on his hand-tooled leather belt. Then he flashed Lo a quick smile.

She smiled back, tucking her red hair behind a delicate ear in an inviting way that made Max want to kiss the lobe. Suddenly, her face fell. "You mean they just let him in?"

Him who?

Max sat up straighter, wishing he didn't feel so bushed from the flight back to Kennedy. Of course, over dinner he'd told Lo he'd spent his day off at Jones Beach in Jersey. Not that she'd believed him. Hell, maybe she was right not to. He was every bit as much of a liar as she was. By pretending to be her bodyguard, he was probably endangering her. And he hadn't been anywhere near Jones Beach. He'd been with Zach, Sheldon Ferris and her grandmother.

Max just wished he knew who was on the phone. Absently rubbing the light stubble on his chin, he listened to Lo say, "The *man?* Uh…you're sure about that? And then what? Not really!"

Suddenly, Lo stared at Max. Covering the mouthpiece, she whispered, "Please. Privacy."

Instead of leaving, Max rose and sidled next to her. He leaned against the counter—so close that he could smell how the scent of her floral perfume mingled with salon shampoo and wood smoke from the steaks they'd just cooked on the grill.

Lo gaped at him.

He crossed his arms over his chest. She wanted him to leave the kitchen and he knew it. But that meant the conversation was probably important. Maybe it was a banker calling about her overseas accounts. Or her accomplice.

Or her grandmother.

Max winced as Gran's voice boomed through the receiver. It was so loud, he was surprised he hadn't heard it from his seat. Had he really sworn he'd return to the Fountain of Youth nursing home to help Josephine Lambert make her great escape? Some days Max really hated himself.

Apparently, Lo had given up on trying to keep her call private. "Can you describe him?"

During the long pause that followed, Max held his breath. What if Gran's description identified him as her visitor? He glanced down. Shoot. He was wearing the same clothes he'd worn to the nursing home. Gran knew he'd come from Connecticut, too, even if he hadn't introduced himself by name.

"Gran?" Lo prompted.

"All I know," Gran shouted, "was that he said he was going to marry you."

Lo clutched the phone so tightly her knuckles turned white. "Please. Don't you remember what he looked like?"

"How would I know?"

Lo glanced nervously at Max and twined the phone cord around her fingers. Maybe she thought the visitor had been a lawman from the FBI or SEC.

When her strap slipped from her shoulder again, Max leaned and slid it into place. Loving the way her silky skin and hair brushed his hand, he let the touch linger, delivering a gentle, squeezing caress. Not that Lo seemed to notice.

"Gran?" she prompted. "Did he have dark hair?"

"Maybe."

"Blue eyes?"

"I don't know. Maybe."

Lo probably suspected Sheldon Ferris had shown up at the nursing home, Max realized, straining to hear Gran's voice, which had dropped.

"I took off my glasses," Gran suddenly shouted. "I didn't want your fiancé to think I was both blind *and* deaf. But I do remember...yes, I think he was handsome. And he didn't have gray hair. I remember that because..." Now Gran's voice rose to a wail. "Because around here, in this *awful* nursing home, everybody—and I do mean *everybody*—has gray hair."

At that, Lo fell apart. "Oh, Gran," she moaned, "I knew I shouldn't have left you there."

"You certainly should not have!" Gran agreed.

Lo flung out her hand, clutching the edge of the countertop for support. "Is it really so bad?"

Realizing his lips were parted in barely contained protest, Max clamped them shut. Gran was probably getting a pedicure while she talked to Lo. Or soaking in a hot bubble bath.

Pathetic little sniffles came over the wire. Then Gran crooned, "Oh, please. Don't give me one single thought. It's really not so bad. It's just that the food portions are so small that...that I may be losing a little weight. Wasting away, really, if you must know. And that Cassie person, my nurse, is—"

"Is what?" Lo demanded sharply.

"Well, she brought that strange man to my room."

Lo's eyes narrowed. "The man who said he was my fiancé?"

"Yes. And just think, Lo. That man could have been *anyone.*"

But he wasn't. He was Max. And just looking at Lo's distressed expression was making Max feel guiltier than ever. Surely Lo thought Sheldon had been interrogating her grandmother. Of course, that meant Lo had really never contacted Sheldon. Which probably meant she no longer cared for him.

"You're right," Lo murmured softly. "It could have been anyone."

"Anyone!" Gran repeated. "Why, that man searched through everything—my pictures, for instance. And now all my clothes are a mess!"

Lo gasped. "Your clothes?"

"Well, he said you were getting married, so I thought he'd come to take me to your wedding."

Lo's voice turned angry. "I promise I'll get you out of that awful place if it's the last thing I do. Gran, you've got to hang in there. I know it's hard, but I love you. And I will be there, I promise. Are you okay? Really?"

There was a long pause. Then a disappointed, if more honest-sounding, Gran said, "I guess. Agnes from down the hall is coming over to watch a rerun of 'The Golden Girls' on my TV tonight. And tomorrow we signed up for a minivan ride."

"Love you," Lo said.

"Love you the most," Gran said.

Within seconds, Lo had redialed the Fountain of Youth to lodge a complaint against Cassie. Fortunately, Cassie was so upset, her description of Max was no better than Gran's.

Lo slammed down the phone. "Some man *was* there. And that awful Cassie woman left my poor grandmother alone with him!"

Max stared at Lo, desperately wanting to defend himself and Cassie. But no, Max was going to get his story. He always did. Even if the angry tears in Lo's green eyes were making him feel lousy about it. Doing the only thing he could think of, Max whispered, "C'mere, honey," and drew Lo against his chest.

A second later, she was sobbing on his shoulder, talking incoherently, letting it all out. No doubt the jag had as much to do with hormones as the conversation with her grandmother, but that didn't stop Max's heart from wrenching.

And maybe his own hormones were doing a little talking. Because as he held her—bending his knees, leaning into her, wrapping his strong forearms tightly around her back—he was sure a woman like her couldn't commit a serious crime. And yet he knew he was reacting to her proximity, to the way her silk sundress teased his bare chest and her tears tickled his skin. The heat of her warmed the already warm length of him.

Yeah, Max thought. *This is physical, not logical. And if you've got any more doubts, just talk to Zach again.*

Nevertheless, as he swayed against the kitchen

counter, rocking her, he fought the insistent urge to tell her that Gran was fine and that he really wasn't a bodyguard. He wanted to say he was Max Tremaine—and he was crazy about her. But then Zach was a force to be reckoned with. And if the P.I. said Lo was guilty, she probably was. Sheldon Ferris had been pretty convincing, too.

As Lo's sobs subsided, her words became coherent. "Gran has spun some kind of rosy fantasy." Lo gazed up, her wet green eyes glittering like jewels, a stray tear rolling down her cheek. "I don't know who visited her, but Gran must have gotten confused. Since she—" Lo broke off and sniffled. "Since she wants me to get married, she's invented a fiancé. Oh, I—I'm never going to get married."

Max nuzzled her cheek. "Sure you will."

"No...I don't even want to. I've had it with men. They're all liars and cheats."

Including me. "No, all men aren't like that," Max said soothingly. He hugged her tight, then rubbed circles on her back until his palms came to rest at the small of her spine. Suddenly, the baby kicked. Lo's eyes shot to Max's.

He winked. "This time, I was expecting it."

That got a smile out of her. "No, *I'm* expecting it."

Max's mouth quirked at the bad wordplay. And yet, as he'd felt that soft kick against his belly, Max's heart had wrenched again. Just this morning, beside Lo's bedroom door, he'd noticed a small green suitcase she kept packed for the hospital. More and more, he'd been wondering about the baby—whether it was a boy or girl, when exactly it would be born.

Not that the questions would be answered. Because—just like whoever had hurt Lo in the past—Max *was* lying. And Lo was bound to find out eventually that he'd used her for a story. Max lifted one of his shirttails and dabbed at her eyes, wishing they didn't hold so much trust. "There you go, honey," he said.

"I had every reason to believe I was putting my grandmother in a really nice place," Lo murmured. "I saw a brochure and talked with them on the phone. And it's so expensive."

Lo was right about that much. Max winced, thinking of the bills. "Maybe the conditions aren't quite as bad as your grandmother makes them sound."

"Gran wouldn't lie," Lo said defensively.

How could a criminal be so gullible? Josephine had Lo utterly snowed. Max said, "Well, maybe she just stretches the truth."

Lo raised her eyebrows. "You think so?"

I know so. Max nodded. "Yeah."

Lo looked relieved. Not that Max was. Why in thunder had he sworn he'd go back and rescue Josephine? He had a sneaking suspicion there weren't many worse places to be than on Gran's bad side....

A nearby crash startled him.

Jarred from his thoughts, Max whirled toward the sound. Just as glass shattered, he grabbed Lo and hit the floor, covering her body with his own. From under the table, he watched glass raining down on the linoleum.

Lo looked terrified. "What's..."

"I think it was a gunshot. I've been in enough war zones that I've heard a few." Apparently, he was wrong about the person threatening Lo. Whoever it was meant business. Max strained to hear a sound in the silence—until something started rolling toward them across the floor. "A bomb," Max murmured. Had one been tossed through the window?

Suddenly, Lo stretched her arm above her head and grabbed the object. "Hate to say it, Boots," she said throatily. "But this looks more like one of Timmy Rhys's baseballs than a Molotov cocktail."

Max groaned. "And I thought I was saving your life."

"Well, look at the bright side."

"What's that?"

"You could still kiss me."

Max straddled her. "Kiss you, huh?" he said. And then he did. Hotly. Wetly. Deeply. Until she squirmed beneath him and said, "We'd really better stop now."

"Because?"

"Because it's now or never."

Max chuckled. "I vote for never."

"If it's ever time for never," Lo murmured, "you'll be the first to know."

"I'd better be."

But it wasn't now. Because outside, the pounding of sneaker-clad feet sounded, and Timmy Rhys screamed, "I swear, Mrs. Tremaine, I'll pay for your window."

8

When Fantasy and Reality Collide...

MAX OPENED ONE EYE. T-shirt stared back—eye to eye, nose to nose. When Max tried to remove him, the kitten merely curled his claws into Max's bare chest. Max grumbled, "Why don't you sleep with Lo?

"No," he amended with a sleepy chuckle, "why don't *I* sleep with Lo?"

Max shut his eyes against the morning light, imagining running the flat of his palm over the taut, butter-smooth skin of Lo's belly. Lord knew, Max had done a lot of things in his life, but he'd never once seen a nude pregnant woman, much less made love to one. And Max loved a novel experience.

He imagined he'd need to be really gentle. But good—because he wanted Lo to forget the man who'd hurt her. "Be honest," he muttered. "You want her to forget *all* men, whether they hurt her or not."

A half sigh, half moan escaped his lips. Maybe one of these days he'd simply walk in on her in the shower. He'd draw back the curtain, then let the thick terry robe she'd bought him last week fall from his shoulders to the floor. Naked, he'd step into the shower with her, the water spray prickling his lower body....

She might blush, but her eyes would trail over him. And he'd let her look—those eyes alone making him ache and burn. Maybe she'd even reach out, twining her damp fingers in the gold hairs of his still-dry chest. Then her hand would inch lower, and lower still, until Max could feel the agonizing pressure of her warm, damp fingers finally curling around his hot, hard shaft....

He could almost see the fat, warm water drops rolling down her. He'd follow them with his eyes—from her wet hair, slicked back from her face, over the tan lines on her shoulders. Sliding the soap bar from her hand, he'd slowly lather every inch of her—her breasts, her arms, her thighs—until frothy white bubbles coated her sun-touched skin.

Later, he'd lift the water massager and train the shocking jolts over her erogenous zones, until she leaned back her head in unbridled ecstasy. His hands would glide through the lather again, over the aroused tips of her breasts, her swollen belly, and then down...down...down, slipping deep between her slippery, sudsy thighs...

"Nah," Max suddenly said.

He'd like it a lot better if they were outside. Someplace far away and isolated. Just the two of them. Alone by a lake, for instance. Maybe it could happen after a picnic. They'd be lying on a red-and-white-checkered tablecloth, feasting their eyes on each other, lazily eating strawberries drenched in heavy cream.

"Definitely." Max sighed blissfully, noticing a trace of cream on Lo's trembling lower lip.

Leaning, he playfully licked it off. She gazed up at him, laughing. Then, all at once, she rose, coyly crooked her finger and turned and fled. As she ran toward the lake, she lifted her sundress over her head. Just as she plunged into the water, the wind caught the dress. It billowed, then rose like a kite—so far into the sky that she could never get dressed again. Not minding, she dipped down, submerged to her shoulders. A second later, she lifted drenched bits of white fabric above the waterline, her bra and panties.

"This isn't a lake," Max murmured. "It's heaven."

He'd follow her into the water, of course. Explore her in the depths. He would learn her whole body by touch alone. Across the smooth, unbroken surface of the wide lake, the only sound would be the lap of water against her skin. Far off, in all that sweet silence, maybe a bird would take flight. But Max would only hear Lo's nearby breathing, and the lapping of the cool, soothing water as it warmed with the heat of their desire.

Suddenly, he heard a big splash—Timmy Rhys's baseball plunked into the lake.

Max chuckled.

No, his best bet was a plain old bed. They'd be doing something ordinary, like sharing dinner at dusk. The last flicker of daylight would dance in her hair—gold in red, like fireflies on autumn hillsides. She'd simply take his hand, and she'd say, "You know how I told you I'd let you know if it was ever time for never?"

He'd say, "Yeah."

And she'd say, "Well, it's time for never."

"No, honey," he'd return, "it's time for *always.*"

"Good line," Max murmured aloud, congratulating himself. Yeah, Lo Lambert definitely brought out the writer in him. Trouble was, it wasn't a line at all. Max really wanted her. Bad. A sharp tug of arousal shot to his groin.

Maybe he should just go down to her room right now. It was a great plan. Why hadn't he thought of it before? Getting up, Max slipped into the terry robe, then headed down the hallway with T-shirt on his heels.

Max would simply tell her how he felt.

Well, maybe he'd emphasize the emotional rather than the physical aspects, since women liked that, he decided, stopping in the bathroom to swish with Listermint. He'd talk about how much fun he'd had assisting with this week's bingo game. And about how cute she'd looked reading to the kids at the library's children's hour. He hadn't even minded helping her baby-sit Colleen's girls, or holding T-shirt while he got his booster shots, since Lo said she'd get teary-eyed. All week long, Max had felt needed. He'd felt touched. He'd felt...

Like he was in love.

There. Maybe he'd even say that. And then he'd steal one of her grandmother's lines, he thought as he headed into the hallway again. He'd tell Lo that if she wouldn't have sex with him right now, she might as well just pick up the telephone and call in Dr. Kevorkian.

"Take mercy," he'd say. "I'm in agony. Pain..."

"No, that won't work," Max muttered. "There's nothing women hate more than needy men." He didn't blame them, either.

Lo. Max almost said her real name out loud. Catching himself, he rapped on her bedroom door. "Max?"

When there was no response, Max pushed open the door. The room was empty, the bed neatly made. And according to a clock, it was far later than Max had thought. Was she downstairs? The kitchen swam into his mind again. He saw himself kissing her, slowly backing her against the table, which was set for breakfast....

"Make love to me," Lo would whisper against his lips.

"Right here?"

She'd nod. "I'm ready."

Max would grab a corner of the tablecloth. As he swept it away, dishes and cutlery would crash to the floor. Then he'd climbed on top of the table, and on top of Lo and...

Downstairs a door slammed, bringing Max back to reality. Lo *was* in the kitchen. Or she had been. Swiftly crossing the bedroom, he peered out a window.

She was leaving!

As his Corvette nosed from under the carport, Max bolted to his room, snatching the first clothes he saw. He wasn't about to let her get away. Zach had called again—this time suggesting Sheldon Ferris could have been her accomplice and then turned on her. Not that there was any hard evidence. But maybe Lo had broken her promise to tell Max where she was going because she was contacting Sheldon. After all, she clearly suspected it was Sheldon who had questioned Gran.

"Just don't lose sight of her," Max growled, hitting the stairs at a hopping run—jumping into cut-offs, shoving his wallet into a pocket, pulling on his boots.

But he was too late! Trying to tell himself he was motivated by a desire for the truth, not jealousy, Max rushed into the street just as his car lurched around a corner. "And she's not letting out the clutch," he muttered.

Well, he was going to find her. He'd find out whether she was innocent or guilty, too. Then he'd at least know what manner of woman lay beneath him if he slept with her.

Not if, he corrected. *When.*

Max glanced around, feeling desperate. Then he realized Timmy Rhys was coming toward him on a small, apple green track bike. Max waved the kid down. When Timmy braked, Max put his hands on the handlebars.

"I need your bike," Max said.

The ten-year-old squinted up, his freckled nose wrinkling. "Uh...I guess it's for rent."

Max groaned. "You still owe me for the kitchen window."

Timmy shrugged. "Price is negotiable."

"Fine." Max whipped out his wallet and slapped a ten in Timmy's palm. "I don't have time to argue."

A second later, Max was wrestling with the little bike—trying to get the deeply treaded front tire to quit wobbling, angling his pumping knees so they wouldn't hit the handlebars, wiggling to find the seat with his larger-than-kid-size rear end.

From somewhere far behind, he heard Timmy call smugly, "I would have taken a buck fifty, Mr. Stover."

It was the only time in his life Max seriously considered killing a ten-year-old. The only saving grace was that the bike was faster than running. And within fifteen minutes, Max found his Corvette parked in front of the local library.

He should have known. Lo was probably planning one of her do-gooder activities—next week's reading program for the kids or a fund-raising drive to buy new books. Maybe she was simply borrowing books on pregnancy, like those she kept around the house. He sighed, thinking he should start trusting her. At least about the little things. Shoot, maybe he ought to just go inside and ask her out for breakfast.

Guess again, Max.

First, she probably wanted lunch by now. And second, he looked like the great unwashed—shirtless, with tousled hair and a scruffy beard. As far as Max was concerned, it was okay that his boxers peeked from beneath the frayed bottoms of his cutoffs. But the underwear was a gift from Suzie, and they had puckered red lips printed all over them. The whole outfit wasn't exactly helped by his cowboy boots.

Or the fact that he was riding a ten-year-old's bicycle.

Max got off and glanced around. Only the landscaping saved the imposing old stone building from looking more like a mausoleum than a library.

Sculpted boxwoods rose from lush, velvety grass, and sprawling rosebushes twined up whitewashed trellises beneath all the windows. Everything was peacefully tranquil. A haven of scholarly decorum.

Max headed for the door anyway.

Behind the circulation desk was a matronly stranger with an iron gray bun. Hanging from a chain, her eyeglasses rested against her crisp white blouse. Slipping them on, she gawked at Max. He smiled back. Through two large, airy rooms, he recognized one of Lo's sweaters, draped over a chair at a reading table.

Iron Maiden looked so scandalized that Max felt compelled to explain. "I came to see my..." What *was* he to Lo? A victim? A lover-to-be? The man who would send her to jail? He settled on "friend."

The librarian sniffed. "It's clear you haven't met Max Tremaine."

"But I am—" *Max Tremaine.* "Looking for Max Tremaine," Max corrected.

Iron Maiden stared at him as if to say the Max Tremaine the community knew and loved would never so much as cross paths with the scraggly likes of him. "Next Monday," she said, "Ms. Tremaine is bringing the issue to vote. Thereafter, shirts and shoes *will* be required, young man."

Young man. It was the second time Max had been called that in a week. He sighed. "I know the boxers look bad, but I've got on shoes and I *am* over thirty."

"Over thirty?" the woman echoed in a hushed tone, her steely eyes flickering over him. "And you dressed in that getup all by yourself?"

"It could be worse." Max flashed her a devilish grin. "I could have left the shorts at home."

Iron Maiden gasped.

And Max headed toward Lo's chair. Just as he realized her reading table was strewn with articles about Meredith and Gersham, he glimpsed Lo. She was coming from the stacks, her nose in a book. She didn't see him. Good, he thought, backing away. He wanted to know what she was up to, but he didn't want her to know he was spying. Maybe he'd climb one of the trellises outside and peek in the window over her shoulder....

Feeling like Indiana Jones at the Temple of Scholarly Tomes, Max planted Timmy's bike against the building, shoved down the kickstand, and climbed.

After a moment, he managed to anchor one boot on the rose-and-thorn-covered trellis, while the other balanced on the seat of the wobbling bike. Stretching for the window, Max tried not to look down at the mess of tangled roses below. He curled his whitening knuckles over the exterior window ledge.

"What am I doing?" he muttered.

He felt like a cartoon character hanging from a cliff. Especially when Timmy's kickstand started rebelling against his weight—sinking in the dirt and forcing the bike to tilt. *Just forget your precarious position and concentrate.* Leaning even closer to the window, he saw that the letters "B.B." were written on Lo's legal pad. Was "B.B." a name? Max wondered. Or was the reference to a B.B. gun? Lo had also written "Arkansas?" and two phone numbers, which Max memorized. Did Lo's research show she was innocent and trying to clear her own name?

Don't get too hopeful, Max. But against his will, his attention strayed to Lo's hair. It was just the way he always imagined it in his fantasies—the soft morning light flecking it with gold. It was the burnished red of autumn leaves and winter fires and…

Her head suddenly turned.

Max froze. *Oh, please, don't let her turn all the way around.* He'd feel like an idiot if she caught him. Shoot. He already felt like an idiot. He strained, trying to sense signs of further movement, and he became conscious of the street sounds—a car horn, a humming motor, a distant siren.

Lo turned back to her legal pad. She wrote and angrily underscored the name "Sheldon." Then she wrote "Setup?" Since they'd been dating, Max was sure Sheldon was the father of Lo's baby, but had Sheldon really let Lo take the fall for crimes they'd both committed? If so, it was a low blow. A double whammy. Max whistled softly.

And then he lost his balance.

A half grunt, half yell escaped from him as his boot slipped from the trellis. The other stayed on the wobbly bike seat, but his hands slid from the window ledge, then snatched at thin air. For a second, Max felt like a high-wire unicyclist in a circus act.

And then it was over.

He landed flat on his back in the prickly rose-bushes. For a moment, Max merely shut his eyes, listening to an approaching siren. *Good,* he thought. *Maybe it's an ambulance.* He breathed deeply, waiting for the pain. When it didn't come, he decided his back might not be broken. Opening his eyes, he groaned. Far above him, the heavy window rolled laboriously upward, its pulleys so ancient that it sounded as if a bowling ball were rolling down an alley.

Iron Maiden's head popped out the window. The siren came closer, sounding every bit as loud as Iron Maiden's shriek. "One look at that man and I knew he was up to no good!"

Lo's head appeared next to Iron Maiden's. Her eyes lingered on his lip-print boxers, then her lips twitched. "He looks like a—a—"

"Hooligan," Iron Maiden finished. "It's a darn good thing I called the police."

Max winced. He was still lying on his back in the rosebushes. Couldn't they just take some pity on him? Besides, if the police questioned him, they'd discover there wasn't really a bodyguard named Boots Stover. "Max," Max called out. "Please tell that woman who I am." As he shimmied gingerly to his elbow, he felt thorny pinpricks on his backside. He guessed it could have been worse. He could have sat on cacti. He glanced up again.

Lo and Iron Maiden squinted down. Lo said, "But I don't think I've ever seen you before."

Max struggled to sit. "But—"

"Don't move!" a woman shouted.

Max ignored the command, moving enough to catch a glimpse of Dotty Jansen. Every bit as pregnant as Lo, the police officer was waddling forth in full uniform—badge out, weapon drawn.

"Move one more time and I swear I'll shoot!" Dotty yelled.

Great. Dotty didn't recognize him. "We would have met at Colleen's on July fourth," Max called out reasonably, ''but you had to work. I swear I'm a good guy. I'm a friend of Max Tremaine's. I'm—''

''Under arrest.''

9

How Two Wrongs Finally Make a Right

"Ouch," Max said.

He was leaning forward, gripping the sides of the sink in the upstairs bathroom while Lo dabbed at his multiple injuries with an alcohol-drenched cotton ball. As she bit back a smile, her eyes drifted over his broad, bare back. Except for the red dots left by the rose thorns, his skin was creamily smooth and evenly bronzed. The wide expanse of his silky, rounded shoulders tapered downward in an enticing V.

"Now, quit complaining," Lo teased.

Max groaned. "I feel like I've been sleeping on a bed of nails. Or used for a pincushion."

"Good. That's what you get for spying on me."

"I wasn't spying."

"Were too." Lo shot him a pointed glance. "Anyway, it could be a lot worse."

"I doubt it, honey," Max returned grumpily.

"Timmy could have found a scratch on his bike. Or Dotty really could have arrested you."

"Oh, please," Max returned drolly. "I was handcuffed and caged in the back seat of her cruiser like an animal before you found it in your heart to tell her who I was.''

Lo laughed. Then she growled like a tiger and pinched Max's back. "You *are* an animal.''

Max chuckled. "Watch it, honey, or I'll turn around and make you better acquainted with my more animal side.''

"Is that a threat or a promise?''

"Ask me one more time and you'll find out.''

Lo's shoulders shook with suppressed laughter. "C'mon," she chided, "I did tell Dotty not to haul you in for questioning.''

"Yeah, at the eleventh hour." Max shook his head. "I just can't believe that lady called the cops—''

"Her name's Mrs. Wold," Lo reminded.

"Hey, she'll always be the Iron Maiden to me.''

Lo tilted the alcohol again, wet the cotton and continued dabbing it on Max's back. "Is that why you promised her you'd vote for the library's new shirt-and-shoes policy?''

"No—'' The breath Max drew through his clenched teeth made a hissing sound. "I promised her my vote because I hate to think of another poor, shirtless guy living in this kind of pain.''

Lo leaned back. "Just hold still.''

"I don't want to hold still.''

She sighed—either because Max was being difficult or because touching his bare back was making her feel so wistful. She just wished she knew if Max had seen the notes on the legal pad that was now safely secured in her oversize handbag. Was it possible he had guessed her identity?

Until today, she'd forgotten about the shoe box in the desk drawer downstairs. Of course, even if Max *had* found her newspaper photo, the picture was as bad as the one Sergeant Mack had and he might not have recognized her. She frowned. Max had maintained a silence about her deception for some time now, and she hadn't a clue as to what he was thinking.

They'd become so relaxed with each other. At times, she almost forgot who he really was—and conned herself into thinking she was Max and he was Boots and they could innocently pursue a relationship. And yet she knew there was something more behind Max's flirtatious expressions. Guessing at what that something was kept her on pins and needles. Still, if Max suspected her real identity, why hadn't he turned her in?

Lo could only hope he didn't anytime soon. All week she'd thought the baby was coming. Of course, it was early, and she'd only been experiencing false alarms. Suddenly, Max's gasp drew her from her reverie. He was glaring at her over his shoulder.

"I never figured you for the leather-and-studs type," he grumbled.

Lo raised her eyebrows. "What?"

"I mean, you're being downright sadistic."

His gaze met hers in the mirror. For a second, Lo couldn't breathe. Like amber whiskey in a crystal glass beside a fire, those eyes warmed her, drifting over her. Lo shot him a sweet smile, then held up the tiny wet cotton ball. "Does this really look like a whip to you?"

Max squinted into the mirror. "More like a chain."

Lo chuckled. "Don't be such a baby."

His mouth quirked. "Just remember that's my tender back you're attacking."

"If I forget, I'm sure you'll remind me." Lo turned her attention to his injuries again, working her way down to where the crinkly elastic waistband of his boxers peeked from his cutoffs.

"*Now* what's so funny?" he said.

"Your underwear."

Max shot another wry glance over his shoulder. "Can I help it if they're in bad taste? My sister bought them for me last Valentine's Day."

"Your sister may have bought them," Lo said. "But you're the one who's wearing them."

Max shrugged. "Shorts are shorts."

But they weren't just shorts on him. "Well, some men wear them better than others."

The remark was meant to be flirtatious, but Lo's voice came out strangled. Suddenly, she was aware of the silence in the small bathroom. And that Max seemed to fill what scant space was left. She could hear his deep, even breathing. And she could smell his bare, sun-warmed skin. When she imagined the salty taste of it, her fingers trembled on his back. Her sharp intake of breath was painfully audible, betraying her emotion, and Max's head tilted as if he was straining to hear her inner thoughts.

Lo mustered an efficient tone. "Well, I guess that about does it." Loudly, she recapped the alcohol bottle and set it on the sink. "Excuse me," she added as she leaned down, reaching past Max's legs to toss the cotton into a wastebasket.

"So you like the way I wear my shorts?"

As Lo straightened, one of her bare knees brushed Max's leg—and a heady, dizzy sensation threatened to cut off her breath. Her swollen belly, suddenly full of butterflies, was still pressing against the man's back, and he was watching her carefully in the mirror.

"Yeah," she managed to say. "The shorts *are* cute."

"Cute?"

Max's level gaze reminded her he was anything but cute. He was all man. All leather and denim and Old Spice. Although he was gentle, sweet and funny, Lo knew those powerful thighs could hold her tight, and those corded forearms might never let her go. She swallowed hard. "Maybe cute's not exactly the word," she conceded as Max slowly turned around to face her.

"Then what is?" he asked huskily.

As she shrugged, he reached up and brushed imaginary strands of hair from her forehead. When both his thumbs dropped down to caress her collarbone, everything seemed to stop. Lo was afraid to move or breathe or even look at him. Maybe it was because of all the lies between them. Or maybe it was just that she was afraid he might stop touching her if she moved.

His thumbs had begun caressing a warm trail on her skin, but now his hands opened, his palms resting flat on her upper chest, the fingers splayed. Her breath caught. She waited for his hands to drop once more, to glide over her breasts—cupping them, feeling their weight.

Max's voice grew suddenly rough with desire, his eyes warm with the heat of it. "I want you," he said in a near whisper. His gaze flickered downward, over her belly. "Can you…"

Make love? At nothing more than that—the unspoken phrase, the mere suggestion—heat seared Lo, charging her nerves, tunneling to her core. "Make love?" she asked aloud, her own voice raspy.

When he didn't immediately answer, her hand rose needlessly, nervously fiddling with her sundress strap. Max made her feel so emotionally naked, exposed.

His finger gently hooked around hers, stopping the movement. His voice was low, almost gruff. "I want to make love to you. But I know the baby's due soon. If it's too late in your pregnancy…"

Lo swallowed against the dryness of her throat. As if anticipating his touch, her nipples constricted against the light yellow summer silk of her dress. Max must have noticed. He brushed a kiss across her lips, while his fingers grazed those taut, sensitive tips with such terrifying tenderness she might have only imagined it.

"It's fine," she managed to say when Max leaned away. "I'm not due quite yet. Even if I was, the doctor said it was all right up until the baby's born. As long as—" color warmed her cheeks "—as it feels all right."

Max angled his head downward. "Believe me," he assured her, his lips brushing hers again. "It'll feel all right."

And she knew it would.

He embraced her then, his strong arms tightly circling her back as his lips pressed hers apart. Without warning, his warm tongue suddenly plunged deep, making the moment explode.

His body was so hard. His chest so bare. And the kiss, such sweet, savage torment. Now, he wasn't asking her if she wanted to make love. He was telling her they would. Each hot thrust of his calculating tongue, each flickering touch of his torturous fingers on her breasts made her burn for him.

Then he shifted his weight against the sink, spreading his legs, drawing her between them until she felt his erection press against her belly. She gasped, never wanting anything more than she did this man at this moment. Vaguely, she realized his silken back had turned hot and slick beneath her hands. Or maybe her palms, which explored the ridges of his muscles, had begun to dampen. Either way, her own flimsy little dress suddenly seemed less like clothing and more like something she'd draped around herself to tease him.

After a moment, he broke their kiss and reached into the cabinet behind them. And then she realized what he was looking for. "We don't have any," she said, wishing her voice didn't sound quite so stricken.

There was another longer, even more stricken pause. Then Max said, "We don't?"

"I'm a pregnant woman without a boyfriend." Lo shot him a wan smile. "Why would I have condoms?"

Max began trailing kisses along her neck. "Because you have a boyfriend now."

"Is that what you are?" she murmured.

Max nodded. "Is this like in that movie *Frankie and Johnny?* You know, where she really has a whole hope chest of Trojans, but she won't admit it because then it would look like she was expecting to have sex?"

Lo laughed softly. "A hope chest full of condoms?"

Max leaned back and surveyed her. "Sure. Michelle Pfeiffer had them in all textures and sizes and—"

"That was *not* in the movie." Lo smiled, never imagining that being with a man could be so easy. "Since I'm not holding out on you, I guess you'd better get going, sailor."

Max groaned. "Why does the guy always have to go on the condom run?"

"One of life's awful little double standards?" Lo suggested. "But since I'm liberated, I'll ride shotgun."

Max playfully caressed her backside. "Next thing you know, you'll have me burning my jockstraps." With that, he grabbed her hand and started tugging her toward the stairs. "You know, this isn't exactly how I imagined making love to you. I mean, not one fantasy began with me falling in a rosebush."

Lo raised her eyebrows. "So you've had fantasies?"

Max's twinkling eyes said there'd been many. "A few."

Lo mustered a Dr. Ruth-like German accent. "Like to talk about them?"

"I'll tell you mine if you'll tell me yours."

She tried to look offended. "You really think I've been lollygagging around all day with nothing better to do than fantasize about a mere man?"

"Yeah." Max pinched her side. "And not just any man. *Me.*"

"So far," Lo admitted, "the reality's exceeded the fantasies."

"Let's see..." Max leaned closer, murmuring against her lips. "So far, you've drenched my back in alcohol, and now we're going condom shopping." Right before his lips closed over hers for another teasing kiss, he whispered, "No offense, honey, but I'm hoping the best is yet to come."

"What's a Trojan?" Jeffie Rhys demanded loudly.

Max's eyes had been fixed on Lo—drifting appreciatively over her dress. Now she watched those luscious amber eyes widen in horror and stare down at Timmy Rhys's five-year-old brother, Jeffie.

"A Trojan's sumpthin' bad, isn't it, Mr. Stover?" Jeffie continued.

Max looked so flabbergasted that Lo took pity and said, "No, Jeffie, they're not one bit bad."

Looking vaguely disappointed, Jeffie shrugged and stared behind the deli counter again. A clerk Lo didn't recognize—a blond, fortyish man whose name tag said Gene—was busy making hot dogs for the Rhys family. Unfortunately, Gene hadn't heard Max ask for the condoms—only Jeffie had.

"Hey, Maxine!" Melvin Rhys yelled from the

back of the store where he and Timmy were getting colas and chips. "Is Jeffie giving you and Boots a hard time?"

Lo shook her head. "Nope."

Then she and Max shared a joint sigh. At Colleen's, Melvin had introduced Max to people as "Maxine's lover," but no one had taken it seriously. Now, Max and Lo were hardly ready to announce what was about to go on behind closed doors. And since the whole neighborhood was in the 7-Eleven, they'd been milling around here forever....

They'd watched Dotty Jansen scrutinize every pretzel and potato chip, unable to decide what might diminish her pregnancy cravings. Then, right before the Rhyses arrived, Slade Dickerson had taken an eternity to choose his lotto numbers. Since there were only four scant aisles in the store, Gene was starting to watch Max and Lo suspiciously, as if convinced they were stealing.

Lo's eyes met Max's again, and they exchanged another desperate glance. Without apology, she took in the way his cutoffs molded his lower contours. The knit shirt he'd put on had risen, showing an inch of his taut, bronzed belly, so she gingerly tugged it down, letting her fingers trace his bare skin. Just that touch made her fingers itch—to tangle in his tousled tawny hair, to lose themselves in the folds of his shorts.

"Not much longer," she mouthed over Jeffie's head.

Max grumpily whispered, "Now Colleen's here."

Lo's eyes shot to the 7-Eleven's double doors. Sure enough, a wood-paneled station wagon had pulled up. Just as all the doors opened like wings and girls in all sizes flew out, Jeffie reached up and tugged Max's shirt again.

"C'mon," Jeffie crooned. "You gotta tell me what a Trojan is, 'cause my big brother, Timmy, let you use his bike."

"He charged me a ten-dollar rental fee," Max protested. When that didn't appease Jeffie, Max continued, "A Trojan's uh...uh..."

His voice trailed off as Colleen's daughters swarmed around him, peering into the ice-cream coolers. His eyes sought Lo's, then moved helplessly to the deli menu. "It's a sandwich," Max finally said to Jeffie. "You know, a Trojan. It's like a hoagie. Or a falafel or a club."

Lo clucked. "A sandwich?" she echoed under her breath as she waved at Colleen.

Colleen waved back. "One ice-cream bar apiece, girls," she shouted. "And no fighting."

"I thought it was a horse," Jeffie said. "So, if a Trojan's a sandwich *and* a horse, is that why people say they can eat a horse?"

"Kids," Max murmured so only Lo could hear. "You gotta love 'em."

When Max's eyes drifted downward, she could feel the heat of his gaze warming her belly as surely as a touch. Then his hand followed in a gentle caress. He was saying he wanted to be a father...but to *her* child? She managed to clear her throat. "Jeffie, I'm not really sure if a Trojan *is* a horse."

"Indeed!" Mrs. Wold suddenly interjected from behind them. "The Trojan horse wasn't a real horse at all. You see, Jeffie, it all goes back to an ancient war between the Greeks and the Trojans...."

The librarian's voice seemed to recede as Lo gazed deep into the golden brown warmth of Max's eyes. Like the last glowing embers of a fire, the lingering glance warmed her to her soul. Max nodded pointedly toward the countless boxes of condoms gathering dust on a faraway shelf behind the counter.

"So close and yet so far," he mouthed.

"And this ancient war," Mrs. Wold was explaining, "was fought for the love of Helen of Troy."

At the mention of love, Jeffie's eyes started to glaze.

Max shook his head. "What a man won't do for the love of a beautiful woman," he remarked to Mrs. Wold.

"So true," the librarian enthused. She glanced approvingly at Max's shirt, her eyes twinkling. "Some might even start wearing clothes."

Max laughed. "Wearing shirts seems safer than starting a war."

Jeffie stomped his foot. "But I still don't know what a Tro—"

"Jeffie," Lo interjected, "I bet Mrs. Wold would love to explain more about Trojans while Mr. Stover and I shop."

"You two go right ahead," said Mrs. Wold pleasantly.

As Lo and Max headed down an aisle, Mrs. Wold's voice rose. "The Trojan horse was really a large, hollow wooden horse filled with Greek soldiers that was driven inside the walls of Troy during the war...."

Max smiled at Lo and draped his arm around her shoulder. "Why didn't we think of that? If only we'd stormed the 7-Eleven in a Trojan horse, I could have leapt out, gotten the con—"

"Gladdy and I *do* hope we'll be seeing you at mass this week, Maxine!" Helen Millhouse interrupted brightly. She swept toward them down an aisle, adjusting the bright blue, wide-brimmed summer hat that covered her hair.

Gladys followed Helen, fanning herself with a lace handkerchief. "It certainly is hot today," she remarked as she passed.

Fixing Gladys with a solemn expression, Max caressed Lo's side. "It seemed much hotter a little earlier in the day."

"It did, Mr. Stover," Gladys said agreeably. "It most certainly did."

Max suddenly chuckled. "Any particular reason we've stopped by the spices again?"

Lo thought of the warm, peppery heat of his embraces and the tangy spiciness of his kisses. She shook her head. "No. Anything we really need?"

"Yeah." His hot gaze flickered over her. "I need you."

"I mean food."

A deep laugh rumbled in his chest. "If you're good, I'll fix you one of my famous Trojan sandwiches."

Lo's laughter was tempered to a smile as Max's hand slid down her back and resettled on her waist. They started walking again, their strides evenly matched. Then he leaned close and kissed her ear. "I do intend to eat you up, you know."

Lo murmured, "Sounds dangerous."

Max's eyes turned somber. "Honey, this *is* dangerous."

Time suddenly seemed to stand still. The air seemed heavier, thrumming with the low-voiced conversations all around them. They really were in dangerous territory. And in this crazy landscape, it was hard to tell which road led to the land of happily ever after—and which to heartbreak.

Lo tried to clear her throat and couldn't. "I've never felt this way before." She was so thirsty for him, and it wasn't the kind of thirst that just one drink could quench.

Max stared at her. "Not even with your...your ex?"

Sudden, flinty anger rushed in on Lo—anger at herself for all the lies she'd told him. But just as her lips parted to spill her secrets, an image of Father Burnes from St. Mary's swam into her mind. *Forgive me, Father, for I have sinned,* she imagined herself saying. Then Lo glanced around the aisle at the stacked jars of mustard and mayonnaise and relish.

Somehow, the 7-Eleven didn't seem like the right place for her heartfelt confessions.

Besides, she'd committed so many sins that if she confessed now, she'd be saying Hail Marys right up until kingdom come.

And she'd lose Max.

Maybe the greatest sin of all was that she didn't even want to be good and confess. All she wanted was Max. He must have been thinking the exact same thing, because he said, "Look, maybe we should just go to another store where we don't know anybody."

Lo nodded. "Well, we can't hide in the relish all day."

Max laughed. "I relish you."

Groaning at the bad pun, Lo glanced toward the front of the store. Gene was ringing up Melvin's purchases. Colleen and her brood were behind Melvin. And Helen and Gladys, each carrying a box of high-fiber cereal, brought up the rear.

"Good," Lo murmured, "we're almost home free."

"Yeah," Max said. "Except Gene's staring at us like we're Bonnie and Clyde."

Lo laughed and pointed at a bin of plastic water pistols beside the door. "Should we stick him up?"

Max smiled. "You hold the gun on him and I'll slide a piece of paper over the counter. Instead of saying, 'Hand over the money,' it'll just say, 'Condoms. Your largest box.'"

"Hey, you, couple in the back—" Gene yelled. He pointed to a No Loitering sign as he finished ringing up Melvin Rhys's purchases. "I've been watching you, and you've been in here for a long time. Were you going to buy anything?"

"Oh, Gene," Colleen quickly interjected. "We *know* them!"

Helen squinted at Lo and Max, then Gene. "I'm sure they just came in for some…"

Gladys picked up the thread. "For some…"

Jeffie's scream suddenly sounded from the back of the store. "For some Trojans!"

LAUGHING, MAX COLLAPSED on the bed, pulling Lo right on top of him. When he caught his breath, he whispered, "Trojans."

"But they're just sandwiches," Lo whispered back.

"Just like a falafel or a club," Max returned.

And then they started laughing all over again—until their eyes teared and Lo was clutching his shoulders. Max could still see Gene gaping slack-jawed at him and Lo in the convenience store. Poor Helen and Gladys had clutched their boxes of high-fiber cereal as if hoping that might make the situation more regular. No doubt Colleen was already phoning everyone in the neighborhood to report the incident.

Between gasping breaths, Lo finally said, "I can't believe we actually held up a 7-Eleven."

Max's shoulders started shaking with merriment again. In the silence following Jeffie's comment, Max had dragged Lo to the bin of water pistols near the door, taking the situation to new heights of absurdity. Once they were armed—Lo with a pink pistol, Max with a blue—they'd loaded the pistols with Evian water from the cooler. Then they'd squirted their weapons in the air. "Hand over the goods," Max had snarled between chuckles, "and nobody'll get hurt." He'd quickly paid for their purchases and they'd escaped out the door.

Now, with a breathy sigh, Lo rolled off him so she was beside him on the mattress. "Well, Mr. Sto-ver—" she surveyed him through narrowed, dreamy green eyes "—I'm not sure I'm still in the mood."

She's so beautiful, he thought, his breath catching. He wanted nothing more than to claim her. Raising an eyebrow, Max said huskily, "Not in the mood?"

Lo shook her head. "I've been laughing too hard," she explained. But her lips, still red and wet and pouty from one of his kisses, curved in a soft, seductive smile that betrayed her readiness.

Propping himself on an elbow, he lithely caught the hem of her sundress, rolled it upward, then lifted it right over her head. As he tossed it to a far corner of the room, the yellow fabric caught the sun, and like a rippling beam of light, it floated to the floor. His voice lowered with emotion. "At least I've finally got you where I want you."

Her voice was raspy. "Where's that?"

"In bed."

Lo sighed with mock boredom. "I guess that's a start."

"Definitely a start," he murmured. Slowly, he caressed her with his eyes, his gaze roaming over her lacy white bra, her swollen belly, her panties. Lifting a finger, he trailed it slowly from her forehead down her cheek.

Ah, why did you fall in love with her, Max? he wondered. He'd fallen hard and fast. Looking at her now, he knew that. Should he come clean? Suggest they pack tonight, go south and hide in Mexico? He tried to tell himself that giving up his career wouldn't be so bad. Every time he looked at Lo, he wanted to quit writing articles, anyway, and start writing poetry. Besides, his bohemian kid sister would love having a fugitive brother.

He sighed. Well, one thing was certain—if he and Lo stayed in the Connecticut suburbs much longer, she'd definitely get caught. *And I can't live without her.*

"What?" she prompted softly.

Max merely shook his head, his finger dropping from her chin to her chest, grazing her collarbone. He thought of his brush with death on his last tour in South America, and how every glance from Lo's green eyes and every breath from between her lips had stirred him back to life on his return.

"From the first moment I saw you," he found himself saying, "I wanted you. My hands wanted to touch you. My mouth wanted to laugh with you...kiss you...taste you." And, oh, his eyes had wanted to watch. To see her turn wild beneath his caresses. To see her face when he thrust into her, forcing rippling pleasure through her.

Her words were barely audible. "I'm feeling a little bit more in the mood now."

Max pierced her with his gaze, his eyes saying what his lips couldn't yet. That he wanted her more than a little bit. He wanted all of her—body and soul. And he was going to demand he got it. His voice caught. "A little bit's not good enough."

"I want you a lot," she corrected.

But, Max, you've been lying to her. You've been taking mental notes on every damn moment you've spent with her, so you could turn her in and break the story. He swallowed against the dryness of his throat, against his guilt. He'd lied for a lark. For a story. Lied, thinking he might easily seduce her—which he had. And all along, she'd thought he was her damn bodyguard. Well, at least he hadn't gotten her killed.

Yeah, you're a real mensch, Max.

Shoving aside his thoughts, he unclasped the front

of her bra, gently opening it, pushing aside the cups, his eyes drinking in her breasts. Leaning down, he drew one into his mouth, then the other. Lavalike heat pooled in his lower belly, then he felt a swift, undeniable tug of arousal. A soft hum thrummed in his chest as he kissed her breasts, his palms gliding over her, touching her everywhere—her rounded belly, her lightly tanned calves, the curving insteps of her feet.

"Maybe if we start here," he murmured, still suckling her, "one thing will lead to another."

"Do you really think so?"

But already her eyes were shut and she was starting to writhe beneath the ministrations of his mouth. Against his lips, her nipples formed pebbles, hardening as he tugged them. His hands drifted down, stroking her intimately.

And then her hands found him. The way her fumbling fingers teased his burgeoning zipper made it obvious she hadn't had many lovers. Her touch was almost more than he could bear; torturously sweet and dangerously endearing, it made him feel full. Heavy. Like he couldn't hold back. Like he was about to explode.

He had to claim her. With the deep rumble of a groan he could no longer contain, he set about doing just that. She craned her neck to meet his lips, and while he removed their remaining clothes, he captured her mouth in a wet, hard, possessive kiss. When he came free of his slacks, he knew he couldn't restrain himself long. He was about to burst.

"I need to be inside you," he whispered, rolling away just long enough to put on a condom. Then, kissing her with unspeakable tenderness, he maneuvered himself above her, then beside her, never breaking the kiss but still searching for a position....

He could feel her tense with apprehension and knew she was experiencing a sinking realization that this wasn't going to work. "It's okay," he whispered soothingly between kisses.

She groaned softly. "But it's not."

"It will be, honey," Max assured her, "because I'm a real patient man."

And he was. Still, no matter how they turned and twisted, it didn't seem right. She was just too pregnant. Pressing a blistering kiss against her lips, Max finally turned her on her side, his warm hands caressing her as he helped her move. Gently, he started to edge in behind her.

Lo's relieved sigh spoke a thousand words. "Maybe this'll work."

Max's answering chuckle was barely audible. "Don't be so nervous."

"Don't be nervous?" she whispered back. "You know, I don't exactly do this every day."

"That's all right..." He trailed hot, wet kisses along her side. "I'm the kind of guy who'll settle for every other day. Unless I'm provoked."

"Am I provoking you?" she murmured.

"Oh, yes," he said, sighing.

And with that, he edged even closer. When his hard length grazed her silky backside, he felt her flesh quiver. Gently, he guided himself to her. Then for a sudden, stunned second, Max couldn't breathe. Lying on her side, Lo was so yielding and vulnerable to him—so open. His chest squeezed tight, his heart so tender.

With his face buried in her neck, he released a final low-voiced moan as he entered her—slowly, carefully—thrusting deep, deep inside.

"Wait," she gasped. "I've never..." *Had a man love me from behind like this.*

Her unspoken words hung in the air as Max blew on a string of kisses he'd left on her skin. "Just lean—lean back against me," he whispered brokenly. "Just lean like you're sitting in my lap...." He guided her with his hands and voice and heart until she found a rhythm that silently pleaded with him, begging for his slow thrusts to turn wilder, deeper, harder...

And then he was lost. Over and over she sank silkily onto him, the soft flesh of her backside molding to the cradle of his lap. It no longer mattered that a world of lies lay between them. With each agonizing thrust, Max realized all that mattered was the love they shared.

They peaked together. Their faces, cheek to cheek, were molded together. Each of them gasped—and as that shared moan passed between them, they felt a shared joy. A shared silence, away from the rest of the world. Because this moment was all their own.

For a long time, Max felt the sweet spasms of her orgasm—holding him and letting him go, mixing with the warmth of his own pulsing climax—and he tried to block out that moment when he would have to tell her the truth. He suddenly wished he'd never come home. And wished he'd never lied.

Because he loved her so much. And he knew the right thing to do was to turn her in—and let her go.

10

The Truth Will Always Out

OUTSIDE, THROUGH THE OPEN screened top of the kitchen's Dutch door, Lo could see an early morning haze lifting to reveal promising blue skies. "Not a single cloud in sight," she murmured.

Maybe Max would keep sleeping, so she could take their breakfast back upstairs to bed. With a satisfied sigh, she tightened the sash on her long, pearl white robe, refilled T-shirt's kitty dish, then turned her attention to the counter and began whisking eggs in a crockery bowl. Through the screen, she heard a bird chirp, then a car door slam. Listening to the bacon sizzling in the nearby skillet, she swung around and snatched up two bread slices just as they popped from the toaster.

When the baby kicked, she smiled. Surely she'd go into labor soon. And if she could only find some hard evidence to clear her name, maybe Max could become part of her and the baby's life.

Max loved her. He'd told her so last night. When he'd first whispered the words, she'd been nearly asleep, drifting in a heavenly netherworld of sensation—breathing in his scent, feeling the warmth of his arms wrapped around her. "I love you so much," he'd whispered. And even if he hadn't, Lo would have known by the way he'd held her—like something precious he'd cherish forever.

Humming softly, she glanced toward the door again—and gasped. The morning buzz in the air seemed to cease, and her hand stilled on the whisk. Carefully setting down the bowl, she turned around slowly, clutching the edge of the stove.

"What are you doing here?" she whispered.

Sheldon Ferris merely stared at her through the screen.

He was as handsome as always—his blue eyes stark against his tan, his dark hair neatly trimmed. But now Lo knew who he really was. And fear, loathing and murderous anger tangled inside her.

Then she thought of Max.

"Great," she muttered, glancing toward the stairs. If Max came down, she was in real trouble. *Hey, honey,* she imagined herself saying, *I'm wanted by the police, in case you haven't put two and two together. But don't worry, with time off for good behavior, I'm only looking at ten to fifteen. And by the way, I'd like you to meet my ex-lover, the father of my baby and the man who got me into this mess....*

"Cat got your tongue?" Sheldon asked silkily.

"My tongue's quite intact. So you'd better get away from that door." When he didn't move, Lo stalked toward him. As she barreled onto the porch, she saw his gray Porsche in the front driveway. Then she realized his eyes were flickering over her nightclothes. Following his gaze, she nearly tripped over the robe's hem.

"Sure you don't want to invite me in for breakfast

and coffee, Lo? I'd hate for the neighbors to see you in nothing more than a negligee and robe."

She ignored him and kept moving—backing him right down the porch steps and then beneath the carport. Another two steps and he would have landed inside Max's convertible. "How did I ever fool myself about you?"

Sheldon's smile didn't meet his eyes. "So you're not going to invite me in? Afraid your latest lover might find me consorting with you in his kitchen?"

"Consorting?" Lo gasped. When Shel's eyes drifted over her belly, they held no surprise at how far along she was. That the baby didn't matter to him chilled her, but she kept her gaze steady. "Consorting?" she repeated. "You're just lucky I haven't killed you—yet."

"Ah," Sheldon murmured, "So Max Tremaine *is* your lover."

Her mind raced. What could Sheldon know about her and Max? "Don't assume you know anything about my relationships."

"Maybe I know more than you think I do."

She knew she should be accusing him, getting him to confess that he had set her up. But with a sudden rush of temper, she said, "You don't know *anything* about relationships. You're incapable of them."

"The SEC would disagree." Sheldon's eyes challenged her. "They feel I'm successful at all my undertakings."

"Oh, you're the picture of success." And he was, with his tailored gray suit, perfectly combed hair and boyish face. "But you're willing to climb over anything in your path to get where you're going, including your own unborn child.''

Sheldon glanced pointedly at the house. ''The way you sleep around, did you really expect me to believe that baby's mine?''

''Not yours?'' Lo stared at him slack-jawed. ''You really are the lowest of the low.''

''Don't push me.''

''Don't push *you!*'' She sank against a column of the carport for support. ''You set me up—''

''Don't blame me for crimes *you* committed.''

His smug smile was making her blood boil. ''We're alone. Are you going to lie even when no one else can hear?''

''I'm not lying.''

''Months ago, your lies ruined my life!'' Lo burst out. ''And now, here you are, destroying my life again.'' She suddenly wanted to hit him—and hard. ''What are you doing here?'' she demanded. ''How did you find me? And what do you want?''

Swiftly, he traversed the scant space between them, trapping her against the carport's supporting column. Rawboned terror shot through her. Why hadn't she seen past this man's pretty-boy facade to the vast emptiness beyond? She suddenly realized Sheldon Ferris was capable of anything.

Including strangling her.

Just as his fingers closed around her neck, she opened her mouth to scream for Max. And then she imagined herself saying, *Honey, could you do me a little teeny favor? Could you just write up a big front-page article for the* New York Times, *explaining how I fell in love with and got pregnant by a psy-*

chopath? And, gee, maybe I can clip it and send it to Gran. Oh, hon, she'll be so proud, I'm sure.

Lo decided to keep her mouth shut.

But Sheldon's hand was still on her neck. It was loose enough that she could breathe, but she felt dizzy. As the world slid off-kilter, only the rigid column pressed against her back kept her upright.

"I came here," Sheldon said, "because I want to know exactly what you've told him."

Oh, no. He thinks Max and I are working together to clear my name. Her voice was strangled. "Told who?"

Sheldon's lethal stare said she'd better start talking, and fast. "Max Tremaine."

"Max who?"

"Tremaine." He ground the name out. "You're *living* with him."

Sheldon was afraid, Lo realized. And she was dead meat if she let on that Max wasn't helping her, that she was still the only person who knew Sheldon had framed her. Judging by Sheldon's grip on her neck, he didn't intend to get caught anytime soon. But to what murky depths would he sink in order to keep her quiet? Lo suddenly imagined herself perched on the Brooklyn Bridge while he affixed cinder blocks to her feet.

She'd remain calm, of course. Perhaps before she took the final plunge, she'd scrutinize the cement slippers. In a husky Greta Garbo voice, she'd say, "Not my style, darling. I prefer shoes from Bloomingdale's and Saks."

Sheldon was losing patience. "What did you tell him?"

Trying to stall him, Lo said, "How did you find me? Were you the guy who went to see my grandmother in the nursing home?"

"No." Sheldon glared at her, his lips curling back from his teeth. "Your boy Tremaine dropped by to see me. He also sicced his P.I. dog on me. Zach Forester's been camped out in my office all week." Sheldon's eyes turned crafty. "But I'll figure out what they know. I can't afford bad press in the *Times*. And I can't have that Zach guy snooping around."

In spite of the fact that a lethal hand was tightening on her tender flesh, relief rushed through Lo. The calls Max said were from the agency were from a P.I. Max already knew who she was—he'd gone to see Sheldon and was probably trying to clear her name. Maybe Max even had hard proof she was innocent. But why hadn't he told her he knew her true identity?

"Did you hear me?"

At Sheldon's low-voiced growl, Lo snapped back to reality. "What?"

"I said I came with an offer."

That was rich. "I think it's a little late for us to take up a peace pipe."

"Maybe. But here's the offer—you get out of town and I don't tell the cops where you are."

In a flash, Lo imagined herself leaving town—and Max. Not to mention her obstetrician. "I can't!" she howled. "I didn't do anything wrong. You set me up. You ruined my life. You made it so I can't even go get Gran. And then you come around threatening me! Get your lousy hand off my neck!"

Instead, the fingers tightened.

She gasped. ''Sh-Sh-Sheldon, you maniac, you're cho—'' She began coughing.

And then, out of the blue, another hand appeared. This one clamped down on Sheldon's shoulder and sent him flying backward with such force that he almost toppled inside the convertible. As the metal taps on his fancy shoes clattered across the concrete, he started to fall. But then he caught himself in the nick of time and saved the knees of his expensive trousers.

''Get out of here,'' Max said simply, ''or I'll kill you.''

''I'll call the cops on her,'' Sheldon warned as he started edging past Lo.

''Since you know where she is,'' Max challenged, ''why *haven't* you called them?''

Sheldon's guilty silence served as his confession. Trying to regain some semblance of dignity, he straightened his tie as he continued edging toward his car. Max followed him, staying just close enough that Sheldon wouldn't think of going for Lo's throat again. Then Max stood in the yard, hands on his hips, until Shel drove away.

Feeling righteous, Lo rubbed her bruised neck. Then she suddenly sighed in relief. *Everything's all right.* She couldn't quite believe it.

Max knew who she was. Both he and a P.I. were onto Sheldon Ferris. A smile brightened her face. And then broadened—because she realized Max was clad only in red boxers printed with big white hearts. No doubt the shorts had arrived in the same Valentine package as his lip-printed ones.

"Everything's really going to be okay," Lo murmured aloud, feeling stunned. Max loved her. He was helping to clear her name. She and Gran would be reunited. The SEC would arrest Sheldon. And some entrepreneur would probably reopen the Dreamy Diapers plant.

Max turned and started toward her. "Oh, Max!" she exclaimed as her feet took flight. When she lunged into his arms, he caught her. Just as suddenly, he let her go.

"Max?" he echoed.

Staring into his furious eyes, Lo realized her mistake. He might have known she was Lo Lambert, but he *hadn't* realized she knew he was Max Tremaine. She gaped at him as he roughly brushed past her. "Where are you going?"

He didn't so much as glance at her. "To pack your bags."

MAX COULD FEEL those green eyes on his back. Not that he'd turn around. Instead, he hauled a matching six-piece set of luggage from a hall closet into her bedroom. One by one, he opened the various cases— including an oversize steamer trunk—and tossed them onto her bed. Then he opened her closet door and started stripping the hangers.

Lo sounded as if she was about to snap. "Those are your best suitcases."

"Oh, I've got plenty." Max hauled a handful of dresses to the bed and shoved them into a carry-on. "If there's one thing I've gathered in all my travels—" he headed back to the closet "—it's excess baggage."

"Are you saying *I'm* excess baggage?"

"Take it however you want."

As soon as he yanked open the top drawer to her chest, Max wished he hadn't. His mouth went bone-dry as his eyes trailed over a neat stack of white cotton maternity panties, then a racy little lacy garter number she'd probably bought to remind herself she'd be thin again someday.

Feeling furious, Max slammed the drawer shut. Not that the contents of the next one turned out to be any less disturbing. Max grabbed a handful of slinky nightgowns. Heading toward the bed, he could still feel Lo watching him. He knew which expression she was wearing, too—pleading and pitiful.

If he turned around and looked, he was doomed. Balling up her last nightgown, he threw it at the bed. It landed in the overnight case.

She sniffed loudly. "The way you're treating my clothes, you might as well use garbage bags."

"Since I probably bought your clothes," Max shot back, "I figure I can pack them any way I see fit."

"I'm going to pay you back." When he didn't respond, Lo added, "With interest."

Lord, she was worse than his sister, Suzie. "Don't talk to me in that whiny voice," Max said. "I can't stand it."

"I'm *not* whining."

But she was. And her pleading tone was threatening his resolve. Bending over swiftly, he swept more clothes from the floor, only belatedly realizing he'd packed his own slacks, cutoffs and lip-print boxer shorts.

"Coming with me?" Lo ventured.

Max shot her one quick, sweet smile. "Think of

them as souvenirs.'' When he picked up the pretty yellow dress she'd worn yesterday, his chest squeezed tight. Somehow, he forced himself to drop it on top of his boxers.

Her voice rose. She was starting to sound panicked. "I said I'm going to pay you back."

"Don't bother."

Lo groaned. "What are you so mad about?"

He slowly turned around. Then he strode toward her. "What am I *mad* about?"

As if only now realizing how angry he was, Lo quickly backed against the doorjamb—and Max almost had a change of heart. The silky sash of her long white robe had loosened and he could see the upper portion of her lacy white negligee. Not to mention her breasts. The bodice barely covered those luscious mounds, and Max wanted nothing more than to bury his face between them and nuzzle. But hell, the woman had been playing him like a finely tuned instrument.

He leaned closer, as if to prove he could withstand the proximity. He couldn't. He found himself remembering how he'd loved her last night. And how she'd loved him back. He could feel the silk of her hair as he caught it in fistfuls, hear her needy whimpers and taste the salted honey of her most private crevices.

Her lower lip quivered.

His jaw set. "You didn't even really hire a bodyguard to protect you from Sheldon, did you? Dammit, I really thought you were in danger."

"I was!" Guilty color flooded her cheeks. "Oh,

Max, if it wasn't for you, Sheldon would have strangled me!''

Just hearing Lo call him Max made him livid all over again. "You know what I meant. I thought you were in danger long before this morning." At least a hundred times he'd imagined someone trying to hurt her. He'd been terrified he wouldn't be there to protect her.

"But if you knew who I was," she said, "why didn't you suspect I knew who you were?"

"Because that phone call you made..." *To the agency.* Max was so mortified, he couldn't even say the word "agency" aloud. "That phone call was completely convincing."

Before she could respond, Max swore under his breath and edged even closer, trapping her against the doorjamb. "God, you're such a good liar. I can't believe how you played me. How can I believe anything you say now? You walked right into my house, got to know my neighbors and started robbing me blind while you hid from the law and—"

Lo's eyes turned flinty. "You believe I was engaged in price-fixing while I was at Meredith and Gersham?"

Max felt like a complete fool. "Lying does comes awfully easily to you."

"I was set up! And I admit it, I was willing to do anything to stay out of jail."

Max's voice was murderous. "Even make love to me?"

Lo gaped at him. "Sheldon set me up," she repeated. "It was his way of getting rid of me because

I was pregnant with a child he didn't want—and a way of keeping himself out of jail."

Max's eyes narrowed. Hell, maybe Lo *was* innocent. "So, you're trying to tell me you weren't his accomplice?"

"Of course not!"

For a long moment, they merely stared at each other.

Then Lo's glittering eyes turned hard. "I can't believe you think I'd do something like that. And as far as I know, Sheldon was working alone." Her chin rose haughtily. "Don't worry, Max. You'll have your money as soon as I can get access to my bank accounts."

Max watched the pulse furiously ticking in her throat. Did she really think he cared more about money than her? His voice became a drawl. "Were you going to pay me back before or after your jail term?"

"Believe it or not, I didn't think I would be going to jail. And, fool that I am, I actually thought for a moment there that you were helping me clear my name. What I don't understand now is why you didn't tell me you knew who I was."

There was another long silence. The air seemed utterly still. A scant foot separated them, but emotionally they were miles apart.

"I get it," Lo suddenly whispered in shock. She tried to back away, but there was nowhere for her to go. "You just wanted the story. You're writing an article about me."

Damn. Those green eyes now held so much hurt

that Max almost crumbled. He would have—except she reached out and punched his shoulder.

"You knew who I was," he found himself saying. "Maybe it was you who wanted me to write a story—one favorable to you."

Lo stared at him as if he were a complete stranger. As if she'd just gotten a peek at the man behind the facade—and didn't like what she saw.

Max leaned so close his breath whispered against her cheek. "Under the circumstances," he couldn't help but say, "you've got a lot of nerve to be so self-righteous."

"Just pack my bags," she returned coolly.

"My pleasure."

Max pivoted. Then he strode back to the closet and started tossing out the remainder of her clothes. Drawers banged, hangers rattled. And the more noise Max made, the better he felt.

Oh, maybe she wasn't guilty. But if she wasn't, there was no proof. And either way, no woman had ever taken him for such a ride. All along, she'd known just exactly who he was. Hell, she'd even guessed at his initial motives for keeping his mouth shut.

Initial. That was the key word, though. Because Max loved her now. But as the anger pumped through him, he assured himself he'd get her out of his system somehow.

Max slammed the packed steamer trunk shut, and his hands stilled on the lid. Tilting his head, he listened to the rattling coat hangers, and realized the room had turned awfully quiet. He glanced over his shoulder. And then he turned fully around.

Lo was gone.

She'd left, wearing only her robe. And she'd taken just one bag—the green suitcase she kept by the bedroom door for her trip to the hospital.

"JUST GO HOME, TIMMY!" Lo shouted.

Darn. She looked a sight. Like the neighborhood crazy lady. Blinking back tears and trying to ignore the hysteria bubbling in her throat, she set her little green suitcase on the pavement, firmly tucked her revealing negligee beneath her long, cumbersome white robe, then tightened the robe's sash over her swollen belly. There. That was a bit more dignified. Bending, she gripped the suitcase handle in a perspiring palm again. And then, trying to block out Timmy Rhys, she headed on down the road. She just wished the sun wasn't beating down on her head. And that she had her Ray·Bans.

After a long moment, she stopped, whirled around and stared over her shoulder. Timmy had pulled his bike onto the edge of Dotty Jansen's lawn. Even from here, Lo could see he looked worried.

Not that she blamed him.

She was starting to feel a little worried herself. She felt all wrong inside. Crazy and heartbroken—as if she really might lose her mind.

The way you just lost Max.

With a sudden tearful yelp, Lo glanced down at her bizarre outfit, and her eyes blurred. Was it just paranoia or were all the neighbors really watching her? Lo could feel eyes peeking from behind every blind and curtain on the block. Phones were probably ringing off the hook, too.

Which was why she couldn't cry.

And why she couldn't change clothes in somebody's bathroom. If she did, she might confess to being the notorious Lo Lambert. And then... *Everybody will find me out! They'll know who I really am. And they'll all hate me! The way Max does!*

Lo whirled around and started walking again, silent, convulsive sobs racking her shoulders. She concentrated all her energy on holding back the torrent, but her breath started coming in shuddering gasps and her head started pounding.

Suddenly, she choked—and the tears fell.

Oh, Lo, she thought. *Get ahold of yourself.*

But she couldn't. Sob after sob escaped her, punctuated by harsh, raspy moans. Tears streamed down her face, even snaking inside her mouth, tasting salty. Somehow she kept walking. With one hand, she clutched her suitcase as if to save her life. With the other, she swiped at her tear-wet cheeks. After a while, she calmed enough to lift the sash of her robe with trembling fingers and daintily dab at the corners of her eyes.

I'll just change at the very first gas station I come to, she assured herself. *There are three nice new dresses in my suitcase.* Unfortunately, two of them were hopeful size eights. At the thought of how big she'd become, fresh tears leaked from her eyes. *Just keep walking. And don't think about Max.*

Timmy's shout sounded from far behind her. "Hey, are you sure you're okay, Mrs. Tremaine?"

That made her cry even harder. Not only was she not okay, she wasn't a Mrs. anything. And she'd sure never be a Mrs. Tremaine.

Lo didn't stop to turn around. She pulled in a deep, tremulous breath and then, exhaling, called, "I'm fine!"

"Well, okay," Timmy shouted. "But maybe you'd better put on some clothes."

I should have, Lo ruminated. *I really should have.* But she'd been so mad she'd just grabbed her suitcase and left. She never intended to see Max again, either. He was just like Sheldon, using her to get ahead. Using her for a story. She tried to tell herself she hated him.

But she didn't.

She loved him.

Another sob was wrenched from her. "And it— it—it's so hot," she gasped aloud. They'd just entered the dog days of August, and she was sweltering in her robe. Even worse, it was too long and dragging the pavement like a wedding train. Lo placed a hand on her belly, hoping that might help calm her sobs, and suddenly wishing she had Gran's shoulder to cry on.

And then she heard the siren. It whooped once behind her and fell silent. Turning around, she watched through stinging, scratchy eyes as a cop cruiser pulled to the side of the road. Sergeant Mack, the same officer who'd questioned her and Max, got out and slammed the door. Since she wasn't wearing her floppy hat, Lo doubted he would recognize her from that night. Nevertheless, he *was* staring at her with the kind of serious expression that said she'd broken some laws. As he approached, his dark eyes drifted over her outfit, then narrowed with concern.

"Ma'am," he said gently. "Now, don't get up-set...."

"You mean *more* upset?" A shaky gasp came from between Lo's lips. She swiped at her cheeks again, thinking that if he was supposed to be a cop, shouldn't he see a few clues that she was hysterical? "I—I—I—"

"Just stay calm."

"C-calm?" she managed to say. "I—I am obvi-ously w-weeping."

He nodded carefully. "I did notice that, ma'am."

Lo gulped down another sob, then shakily brushed enough tears from her eyes so she could double-check his name badge. "Don't w-w-worry, S-Sergeant Mack."

"I'm not going to run you in for indecent exposure or anything like that," he assured soothingly, edging closer.

Indecent exposure? She was dressed from head to toe and about to die from the heat of it. "My gown is d-d-dragging on the p-pavement."

"And you *do* look lovely, ma'am."

She didn't, but it was nice of him to say so. Even if he was only being nice because he thought she was insane. Lo clutched her suitcase handle tighter as her belly tensed and another heartbroken sob es-caped her lips.

Sergeant Mack stared at her intently for a moment, then dipped his hand inside his shirt pocket. He with-drew a picture and stared at it, then Lo. He shoved the picture in his pocket again. His hand darted to his holster and hovered there. "My, oh, my," he muttered. "You're Loraine Lambert. We just had an

anonymous tip you'd been sighted in the neighborhood, but I didn't think you were really…''

For a stunned moment, neither of them moved.

The thought flashed through Lo's mind that Max
had actually turned her in. No, it was probably Sheldon. Not that it really mattered now, Lo decided,
dropping her suitcase with a thud. Maybe this was
for the best. In fact, she felt relieved. Without Max,
she didn't care where she spent the next ten to fifteen
years.

Or the rest of her life.

Until she thought of the baby. But by then it was
too late. She'd already stuck out her wrists. ''Just
go—go—go—''

Sergeant Mack didn't budge. ''I'm not going anywhere.''

''Go—go ahead and arrest me,'' Lo finished.

Before she realized that it was actually happening,
Sergeant Mack had clamped on the handcuffs. Seemingly concerned about her condition, he then gently
urged her to the cruiser and all but lifted her inside.
Slamming her door, he circled the car and got in the
driver's seat.

Readjusting his rearview mirror, he squinted at her
and shook his head. ''You sure don't look like the
type to commit a felony.''

Lo stared through the wire-mesh screen that separated the seats. Taking one deep, fortifying breath,
she thought of Sheldon and Max and managed to say,
''Looks can be deceiving.''

Sergeant Mack sighed. ''Do I need to stop for
Kleenex?''

Why did he have to say that? Such kindness from

a stranger just made Lo cry all over again. She clamped her trembling lips together and crossed her arms and shut her eyes tight. But it was no use. Tears squeezed out from between her eyelids.

"I—I'm okay," she croaked. And she almost was—until she turned around and looked at Max's house. Across the street, Timmy Rhys was a tiny dot, pointing excitedly at the cruiser and dragging Dotty Jansen onto her porch. Unlike Timmy, Max probably hadn't even noticed Lo was gone. Maybe he was still angrily packing all her clothes.

Max.

Lo suddenly felt so hysterical she couldn't breathe. "J-just drive."

Sergeant Mack squinted at her suspiciously. "Pardon my saying so, but you've eluded the law for months. What's the rush now?"

Taking another deep breath, Lo shouted, "Just go!"

Sergeant Mack merely peered through the back window, as if to see from whom she was running away. His eyes met hers again. "Why?"

"B-because if you don't—" without warning, Lo doubled over "—you'll be delivering my baby in your b-back—"

Sergeant Mack clearly wasn't registering her words. "Back seat?" he ventured helpfully.

From her hunched position, Lo craned her neck upward to meet his gaze. "I'm in labor!" she shrieked.

The news seemed to hit Sergeant Mack all at once. His dark eyes widened. Then in a swift, simultaneous motion, he whirled around, turned on his siren, grabbed his police radio and stomped on the gas.

FEELING STUNNED, Max stared at the cruiser's receding taillights. He never should have let Lo go outside. Or raced outside after her, he realized when he glanced down. He was still clad only in his red boxers with the big white hearts. Glancing between his car and the house, he couldn't decide which to do first—dress or follow the cruiser.

Or deal with the neighbors.

They were all slowly gathering across the street on Dotty Jansen's lawn. Kids on bicycles were starting to ride in circles in the street and gawk at Max. Max could see Colleen and Dotty and Melvin and Timmy and...

They're all glaring at me.

Wondering why, Max raised his voice. "Did I do something wrong?"

Nobody said a word. The kids on bikes circled closer, and Helen and Gladys headed toward Dotty's, clutching each other's elbows. From far down the block, Mrs. Wold charged right down the middle of the road.

Max watched as Dotty's hands shifted from her swollen belly to what used to be her hips. She headed across the street with fiery wrath in her eyes. Max just hoped Dotty would hurry and say her piece. He had to get to the precinct, and he'd prefer to do so quietly, without the neighbors realizing the true criminal identity of their most upstanding citizen.

Dotty leaned against his front gate. "Did you call the cops on Lo?" she demanded.

"Call the cops?" Max echoed. His first thought was that Dotty *was* a cop. His second was that Dotty already knew who Lo was.

"You heard me, Tremaine."

Guess she knows who I am, too. Not that it mattered. The way Dotty's eyes bored into him, Max could have been wearing a T-shirt that said Max Tremaine, Enemy To All Hormonal Pregnant Women. Out of the corner of his eye, he saw little Jeffie Rhys run up to the wrought-iron fence posts. Jeffie grabbed the bars and scowled through them at Max. The kid looked as if he could win a spot in the Guinness book of Records for world's youngest prison inmate. Max swallowed hard. For all he knew, Lo was already locked in a cell.

Dotty sounded disgusted. "You *did* call the precinct!"

"No, I didn't." Max's jaw slackened. "And I can't believe you knew who she was."

"Do I look like an idiot?" Dotty fumed. "I'm a cop. Of course I knew who she was. Everybody knows. Her picture's been all over the papers for months! Including the *Times,* for which you yourself write. We're just trying to give her some space until I can catch—" Dotty cut herself off. "Oh, never mind!"

Max sighed. "Hey, Melvin," he managed to say when Melvin appeared next to Dotty.

Melvin didn't even bother to respond. He merely grabbed Timmy and Jeffie and started hustling them back across the street. Over his shoulder, he shouted, "Your place used to be a real eyesore, Tremaine. One big abandoned blot on the block. We won't forget it was Lo Lambert who turned it into a show-case.''

"And it's safer for the kids now because of her crime watch program," Colleen added, urging her girls away from Max's yard as if from under the bridge of a resident troll.

Helen and Gladys were still keeping their distance—their postures painfully erect, their arms crossed and their chins in the air.

Max raised an eyebrow. "Anything you two would like to add?"

"Mr. Tremaine, that sweet girl could never commit a crime," Helen pleaded in a tearful voice.

"C'mon," Gladys said, dragging Helen back across the street. "We'll just go inside now. We most certainly will!"

Max's lips parted in mute protest as the two women skedaddled home. Then he thought of Josephine Lambert—and winced. No doubt Gran was still waiting for him to rescue her from the Fountain of Youth. He realized Mrs. Wold was standing stock-still in the middle of the street, staring at his bare chest and clearly trying to think of something suitably nasty to say.

"You are barred from the library forever, young man!" the librarian finally shrieked.

Thankfully, the front door of Dotty's house suddenly swung open. "Honey," Dotty's husband shouted.

Dotty's expression softened the second she glanced away from Max. "Yeah, sugar cube?"

"The precinct's on the phone. Lo Lambert just went into labor. And they need a lady cop."

"Labor?" Max's hands shot to his pockets, searching for his car keys. But of course he was still in his boxers. He stared at Dotty. "I swear I didn't call the cops. And I've got to get to the hospital!"

Dotty's eyes turned steely. "Within ten minutes, I'll have a restraining order. You come within a hundred feet of that hospital and I *will* arrest you." She raked her eyes over him. "Indecent exposure will only be the beginning. I'll book you for harboring a fugitive, your past outstanding parking tickets, which I *do* know about, Tremaine, and—"

"Dotty, you can't be serious. She needs me."

"Like she needs a hole in the head."

"I didn't call the cops. That's crazy. Sheldon Ferris probably called. If I was going to turn her in, I would have done it already. Lo and I have been living here together for—"

"This entire neighborhood has been listening to you two fight all morning. In the carport. Upstairs. In the yard. Pul-lease," Dotty finished.

"Dotty..."

Her eyes narrowed. "Consider that hospital your personal gateway to a holding cell."

For a stunned moment, Max merely stood there in his underwear. And then he did the only thing left to do—stormed inside the house. Lord, his life had sure become complicated since Lo Lambert had barged into it. What in the world was he going to do?

Clear her name, Max.

Without hesitation, he retrieved the file Zach had given him, then headed for the shoe box in the desk drawer, with T-shirt close on his heels. Plunking the box on the desktop, Max started rereading the articles. Words were his business. He knew how to read between the lines. Text, and subtext. In here, somewhere, was something that could clear Lo.

"C'mere," he murmured, lifting T-shirt onto his lap.

After a long time, Max's hand stilled on the car service receipt. When he'd first seen it, it had bothered him. But why? Lo's signature was far too neat to be his own undignified scrawl, but the driver, Jack Bronski, was the same man who'd brought Max home some weeks ago....

Max held his breath. He was close. He could feel it with every journalistic instinct he possessed.

He shook his head, remembering. When he was leaving for South America, the car he'd ordered had never come. Probably Jack Bronski thought he was supposed to bring Max home from the airport rather than take him there. Inhaling sharply, Max suddenly said, "The time."

And then he knew he'd found his answer.

11

How It All Ended Happily Ever After

"FIVE MORE MINUTES—" Dotty Jansen shoved her
hands in the pockets of her police uniform and
glanced stoically into Lo's hospital room, clearly determined not to let her emotions undermine her law
enforcement professionalism. "And then I'll have to
come back for the baby, Lo."

Lo nodded in spite of her tears and stared down
at little Josephine again. The baby was clad in a pink
cotton blanket and a white skull cap that was knotted
on top, and she was curled in a fetal position against
Lo's chest, almost as if she'd never even left the
womb. Named after her great-grandmother, Josie was
completely bald, and as far as newborns went, she
was both long and heavy, measuring twenty-one
inches and weighing nine pounds, four ounces. Already, she had the Lamberts' trademark devious glint
in her eyes, and all the nurses who'd witnessed Lo's
twelve-hour labor remarked that Josie had definitely
inherited her hearty screams from her mother. Josie
was healthy—solid and sturdy and strong. But curled
against Lo, her infant daughter felt like the most fragile thing on earth.

Especially since Dotty was taking her away in only

five more minutes. Lo tried to assure herself the sep-
aration was only temporary. Dotty said the neighbors
would provide character references, so Lo might get
out on bail. And rather than place Josie with child
services while Lo's future was decided, Dotty had
arranged to watch the baby.

Lo glanced at a clock, then through a window. It
was dark out, just after one in the morning. Maybe
she should make a run for it, baby in tow. She was
tired and she ached all over, but she could do it.
She'd find Max, beg him to hide her and Josie.

Get serious, Lo. She could still envision him shoving all her clothes into that big old steamer trunk on
the bed. Yesterday—or was it only today?—he
hadn't even folded her delicates. The sheets and
spread had still been rumpled from the tenderest
lovemaking Lo had ever known. It was the kind of
detail she desperately wished she could forget.

Tears threatened again, but she bit them back. Or
maybe she'd simply cried them all. She sighed. *Why
did I confess?*

Because, she answered herself, *in the throes of a
twelve-hour labor, all women probably lose control.*
It was at the eleventh hour—quite literally—when Lo
had spilled her best-kept secrets. Dotty Jansen had
been hovering over her all day like a kindly nun—
dabbing her sweaty forehead, squeezing her fingers,
murmuring encouragement.

In a spasm of guilt, Lo simply told all—that she
was Lo Lambert, that she was responsible for everyone in the community being out of jobs, that she'd
stolen Max Tremaine's house and car and name and

life. Not to mention ruined the clutch on his prized Corvette.

"Max might have loved me—" Lo's voice had risen to a wail "—if I wasn't the kind of awful person who abandoned my own grandmother."

"There, there…" Dotty had patiently rubbed her shoulder. "We knew who you were the first day you arrived on the block. And I've been doing everything I can to clear you."

And now you'll just have to cling to that, Lo thought, possessively clutching Josie. As her gaze trailed slowly over the little white cap on Josie's head, her eyes filled with tears again. The skull covering made Josie look like the world's littlest cat burglar. "Maybe it's something horrible in our genes," Lo whispered mournfully as she snuggled the blanket around Josie. *Something Max sensed…*

Dotty had told Lo she'd threatened Max with a restraining order. But Max was a professional journalist, accustomed to railroading his way into wherever he wanted to go. If he'd wanted to come to the hospital, nothing could have stopped him.

The door opened.

Lo's eyes remained riveted on Josie, and her arms tightened around the pink blanket. Pure panic welled inside her, and she had a sudden change of heart. *I'm not giving up my daughter! Not even for a minute. Not even to Dotty.* Lo rose, clutching Josie, thinking she'd fight the entire Connecticut police force if she had to. She looked up, her fierce eyes full of newfound maternal fury.

Max stared back.

There was a long silence.

Then he simply plopped the first edition of the *Times* onto the bed. Only one thing could have pulled Lo's gaze away from Max's gorgeous amber eyes: Lo Lambert Cleared Of All Charges.

When Lo's eyes shot from the headline to Max's face again, his unreadable expression made her heart squeeze tight. He'd done exactly what he'd set out to do—written his story. He'd come here because he'd cleared her name, not for her and Josie. Still holding the baby tight, Lo concentrated all her energies on not letting Max see her cry. Her eyes stinging, Lo stared down at the newspaper and tried to look interested.

"Well, Lo..." Even though Max's voice was matter-of-fact, it sent ripples of awareness through her, which she did her best to ignore. "The primary source who tipped me off about you called *before* the warrant to search Meredith and Gersham was ever even issued. I broke the story. Wrote it on my laptop while I was on a plane to South America. But it turns out I had the news a full hour before I logically could have. The car service receipt in the shoe box downstairs made me start questioning the time frame...."

Max waited. When she said nothing, he went on, "I've been running around all night. I found the source who tipped me off. He admitted Sheldon paid him to tell the *Times* you were guilty of price-fixing. By the time the SEC arrived at Meredith and Gersham, I was already collecting secondary sources.

"I also found your assistant, B.B. She got married down in Arkansas, which was why she wasn't listed anywhere under her maiden name, but she wants to come back and testify against Sheldon.

"When I tried to call the hospital, so you'd know, I couldn't get through because of Dotty's instructions." Max dragged a hand through his tousled hair. "Anyway, Sheldon's been arrested in Manhattan— and the D.A.'s made deals with some of his business associates who've agreed to testify against him."

Lo forced herself to look at Max. How could he be so unemotional? He sounded like Hercule Poirot. One more solved crime down. Four to go. She sighed. Max was a great investigative reporter. She had to give him that. Her voice sounded far more stiff than she intended. "Well, thank you so much for coming by to let me know."

Max's eyebrows knit together. "Excuse me?"

"I said—"

"I heard what you said."

God, Lo wished he'd leave. As far as she was concerned, every woman was entitled to a well-earned postpartum depression. And she was starting to crave another good long cry. No one was going to take away Josie. Sheldon had been arrested. Now Lo could go get Gran and access her bank accounts and...

Max was still staring at her. She fought to keep her tone calm and controlled. "I've kept records of my expenditures. And I'll get a check to you."

When Max said nothing, she added, "ASAP."

His eyes had narrowed so much they were nearly closed. "Have I missed something here, honey?"

Lo managed to shake her head. "No, I think that

concludes our business." *I can't believe it. I sound like I'm back at Meredith and Gersham.*

"Business?" Max gaped at her. "Shoot, Lo. I thought you were in love with me."

Suddenly, Lo realized he looked as haggard as she felt. Her eyes trailed over him—from his bloodshot eyes to his uncombed tawny hair and the rough stubble on his jaw. A cigar poked from the pocket of his untucked, wrinkled plaid work shirt. It was wrapped in bright pink paper that said It's A Girl.

It hit her. Max cared about her. He cared about Josie. And all the time she'd been in labor, Max had been busting his buns to clear her name and make the morning edition. Lo's throat squeezed shut and her voice came out strangled. "Do you want to see Josie?"

The next thing Lo knew, the baby was in Max's arms. "I did see her, honey. First thing. When I got here, she was in that—uh—incubator room or whatever they call it. I just didn't want to see you until I had the newspaper in my hands and could convince Dotty not to arrest me. But Josie was the best-looking baby in there. Definitely, the very best." Max finally stopped, then asked, "Don't you love me, Lo?"

"Do you love *me?*"

"Is this a Mexican standoff?"

Lo noticed how comfortable Josie looked, curled against his chest. "I guess it is."

"Look," Max murmured, "I know this is a lot at once. But I just got a message from my sister, Suzie. She eloped with her boyfriend, Amis, to Paris. Anyway, they got back to the States last night and they're desperate for a place to stay. So I was thinking you and I could give up the cottage.''

Feeling a little unsteady, Lo sat down on the bed. Max sat next to her, cradling Josie. Lifting a finger, he trailed it down Lo's cheek.

''We'll need a bigger place,'' he continued. ''And Dotty said Blake and Karen changed their minds again—they're definitely taking the Manhattan condo. So, Suzie and Amis could live in the cottage and we could buy Blake and Karen's place. It's just four doors down.''

''In the same neighborhood,'' Lo murmured.

Max nodded. ''Unless their house moved since I last looked.''

Lo realized she was holding her breath and forced herself to exhale. ''Max,'' she began, trying to keep her voice level. ''That house has got five bedrooms and a garage apartment.''

''Josie needs a nursery,'' he countered. ''And we may want other kids.''

Was he proposing? Or asking her to live with him? ''What would we do with a garage apartment?''

''It's separate from the house—'' Max flashed her a quick smile ''—so I figured we could put your grandmother in there.''

Lo's heart skipped a beat. And then it hit her. Max wanted it all with her. The house in the suburbs. The little white fence. The dogs and cats and kids and Gran. The suburban home she used to dream about would now be a reality. And Lo would have her dream wedding, too.

''You okay, honey?'' Max whispered.

Gingerly, so as not to upset the baby, Lo wrapped her arms around his neck. "I love you, Max."

"Will you marry me?"

"Oh, yes."

The baby squirming between them didn't stop Max's lips from finding hers. He kissed her hard—until she started hoping he'd never stop. After a long moment, he leaned away. Then he called, "Send in my surprise."

The door swung open.

And Josephine Lambert jogged into the room in a nautical blue-and-white warm-up suit. "Ahoy there!" she boomed.

"Gran!" Lo gasped.

Gran didn't respond, merely raced over and flung her arms around Lo. The hug squeezed the breath from her granddaughter and another tear from her eye. Running her hands over Gran's back, Lo sighed in relief. She could feel the wiry, pulsing energy that told her Gran was just fine.

Stepping back, Gran ran a quick hand through her orange hair. Then she beamed down at her squirming namesake. "I *knew* your fiancé would come back for me," Gran enthused.

Lo squinted from Gran to Max. "That was *you* at the nursing home?"

Max nodded, then glared pointedly at Josephine. "And it was *nice* there."

Gran chortled. "Oh, I guess it wasn't so bad—in retrospect." Gripping Lo's elbow excitedly, Gran raced on. "Max says if you marry him that I might get a garage apartment. And Helen and Gladys already signed me up for bingo."

Lo blinked. "You met Helen and—"

"Oh, yes, I've been at the cottage for hours." Gran looked sorely offended that Lo might think otherwise. "Your neighbors are very nice. I just didn't want to burst in on you during labor. I was afraid the shock of seeing me...well, who knows what could have happened! Anyway, the second Josie was born, we all headed over here."

"You came in earlier this evening?"

"Max flew down and personally packed my things and then he brought me back in a little plane they use at some newspaper he works for. Isn't that right, Max?"

"Yes, ma'am. And that little paper I work for is the *New York Times*—"

Gran didn't hear. She was too busy wringing her hands. "Are you going to marry him or not, Lo?" Just as Dotty reentered the room, Gran wrestled Josephine away from Max and said, "Well?"

"Yeah, Gran," Lo replied with a soft chuckle. "Of course I'm going to marry him."

With a satisfied nod, Gran turned so Dotty could admire Josie. "Isn't she a beauty?" Gran murmured. "Just like my Lo. And she's named after me, of course."

Lo shook her head. "I expected to catch hell about getting pregnant."

"And instead you caught me." Max chuckled and leaned close, draping an arm around Lo and nestling her against his side. He winked. "On the plane, I gave Gran a long, detailed account of how happy I'm going to make you."

Lo smiled. "And you bribed her with that garage apartment."

Lo's eyes shifted from Max just long enough to gaze tenderly at the two Josephines—old and young. Sighing, Lo thought about all that lay ahead—meeting her in-laws, the picnics and cookouts and days at the beach.

"I'll reopen the Dreamy packaging plant," she suddenly said. Since she wanted to stay home, at least until Josie went to school, she could become a silent partner, funding the reopening of the plant with all the money she'd saved.

But none of that really mattered now. All that mattered was that her family was here. She gazed deep into Max's eyes—those heart-stopping, soul-warming eyes.

"Everything's perfect," she murmured. "Isn't it, Max?"

"Sure is." He smiled, nuzzling his cheek against the top of her head. "What could possibly be more perfect than you?"

"One thing."

Max tilted his head and caught her lips in a quick, sweet, gentle kiss. "What's that?" he whispered.

"Us," Lo whispered back.

LOVE & LAUGH

INTO AUGUST!

LOVE & LAUGHTER™

Take 4 bestselling love stories FREE

Plus get a FREE surprise gift!

Special Limited-time Offer

Mail to Harlequin Reader Service®

P.O. Box 609
Fort Erie, Ontario
L2A 5X3

YES! Please send me 4 free Harlequin Love and Laughter™ novels and my free surprise gift. Then send me 4 brand-new novels every other month, which I will receive months before they appear in bookstores. Bill me at the low price of $3.24 each plus 25¢ delivery per book and GST*. That's the complete price and a savings of over 10% off the cover prices—quite a bargain! I understand that accepting the books and gift places me under no obligation ever to buy any books. I can always return a shipment and cancel at any time. Even if I never buy another book from Harlequin, the 4 free books and the surprise gift are mine to keep forever.

302 BPA A7TR

Name	(PLEASE PRINT)	
Address		Apt. No.
City	Province	Postal Code

This offer is limited to one order per household and not valid to present Love and Laughter™ subscribers. *Terms and prices are subject to change without notice. Canadian residents will be charged applicable provincial taxes and GST.

CLL-397   ©1996 Harlequin Enterprises Limited

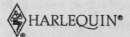

As Seen on TV!

Free Gift Offer

With a Free Gift proof-of-purchase
from any Harlequin® book, you can receive
a beautiful cubic zirconia pendant.

This stunning marquise-shaped stone is a genuine cubic
zirconia—accented by an 18" gold tone necklace.
(Approximate retail value $19.95)

Send for yours today...
compliments of ◆HARLEQUIN®

To receive your free gift, a cubic zirconia pendant, send us one original proof-of-purchase, photocopies not accepted, from the back of any Harlequin Romance®, Harlequin Presents®, Harlequin Temptation®, Harlequin Superromance®, Harlequin Intrigue®, Harlequin American Romance®, or Harlequin Historicals® title available at your favorite retail outlet, together with the Free Gift Certificate, plus a check or money order for $1.65 U.S./$2.15 CAN. (do not send cash) to cover postage and handling, payable to Harlequin Free Gift Offer. We will send you the specified gift. Allow 6 to 8 weeks for delivery. Offer good until December 31, 1997, or while quantities last. Offer valid in the U.S. and Canada only.

Free Gift Certificate

Name: _____

Address: _____

City: _____ State/Province: _____ Zip/Postal Code: _____

Mail this certificate, one proof-of-purchase and a check or money order for postage and handling to: HARLEQUIN FREE GIFT OFFER 1997. In the U.S.: 3010 Walden Avenue, P.O. Box 9071, Buffalo NY 14269-9057. In Canada: P.O. Box 604, Fort Erie, Ontario L2Z 5X3.

084-KEZR

HARLEQUIN AND SILHOUETTE
ARE PLEASED TO PRESENT

Love, marriage—and the pursuit of family!

Check your retail shelves for these upcoming titles:

July 1997
Last Chance Cafe by Curtiss Ann Matlock
The most determined bachelor in Oklahoma is in trouble! A
lovely widow with three daughters has moved next door—and
the girls want a dad! But he wants to know if their mom needs
a husband....

August 1997
Thorne's Wife by Joan Hohl
Pennsylvania. It was only to be a marriage of convenience—
until they fell in love! Now, three years later, tragedy
threatens to separate them forever and Valerie wants only to
be in the strength of her husband's arms. For she has some
very special news for the expectant father...

September 1997
Desperate Measures by Paula Detmer Riggs
New Mexico judge Amanda Wainwright's daughter has been
kidnapped, and the price of her freedom is a verdict in
favor of a notorious crime boss. So enters ex-FBI agent
Devlin Buchanan—ruthless, unstoppable—and soon there is
no risk he will not take for her.

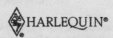 

LOVE & LAUGHTER LET'S CELEBRATE SWEEPSTAKES
OFFICIAL RULES—NO PURCHASE NECESSARY

To enter, complete an Official Entry Form or 3" x 5" card by hand printing the words "Love & Laughter Let's Celebrate Sweepstakes," your name and address thereon and mailing it to: in the U.S., Love & Laughter Let's Celebrate Sweepstakes, P.O. Box 9076, Buffalo, NY 14269-9076, or in Canada to, Love & Laughter Let's Celebrate Sweepstakes, P.O. Box 637, Fort Erie, Ontario L2A 5X3. Limit: one entry per envelope, one prize to an individual, family or organization. Entries must be sent via first-class mail and be received no later than 11/30/97. No liability is assumed for lost, late, misdirected or nondelivered mail.

Three (3) winners will be selected in a random drawing (to be conducted no later than 12/31/97) from among all eligible entries received by D. L. Blair, Inc., an independent judging organization whose decisions are final, to each receive a collection of 15 Love & Laughter Romantic Comedy videos (approximate retail value: $250 U.S. per collection).

Sweepstakes offer is open only to residents of the U.S. (except Puerto Rico) and Canada who are 18 years of age or older, except employees and immediate family members of Harelquin Enterprises, Ltd., their affiliates, subsidiaries, and all other agencies, entities and persons connected with the use, marketing or conduct of this sweepstakes. All applicable laws and regulations apply. Offer void wherever prohibited by law. Taxes and/or duties on prizes are the sole responsibility of the winners. Any litigation within the province of Quebec respecting the conduct and awarding of prize may be submitted to the Régie des alcools, des courses et des jeux. All prizes will be awarded; winners will be notified by mail. No substitution for prizes is permitted. Odds of winning are dependent upon the number of eligible entries received.

Any prize or prize notification returned as undeliverable may result in the awarding of that prize to an alternative winner. By acceptance of their prize, winners consent to use of their names, photographs or likenesses for purposes of advertising, trade and promotion on behalf of Harlequin Enterprises, Ltd., without further compensation unless prohibited by law. In order to win a prize, residents of Canada will be required to correctly answer a time-limited, arithmetical skill-testing question administered by mail.

For a list of winners (available after December 31, 1997), send a separate stamped, self-addressed envelope to: Love & Laughter Let's Celebrate Sweepstakes Winner, P.O. Box 4200, Blair, NE 68009-4200, U.S.A.

LLRULES

Celebrate with
LOVE & LAUGHTER™

Love to watch movies?

Enter now to win a FREE 15-copy video collection of romantic comedies in Love & Laughter's Let's Celebrate Sweepstakes.

WIN A ROMANTIC COMEDY
VIDEO COLLECTION!

To enter the Love & Laughter Let's Celebrate Sweepstakes, complete an Official Entry Form or hand print on a 3" x 5" card the words "Love & Laughter Let's Celebrate Sweepstakes," your name and address and mail to: "Love & Laughter Let's Celebrate Sweepstakes," in the U.S., 3010 Walden Avenue, P.O. Box 9076, Buffalo, N.Y. 14269-9076; in Canada, P.O. Box 637, Fort Erie, Ontario L2A 5X3. Limit: one entry per envelope, one prize to an individual family or organization. Entries must be sent via first-class mail and be received no later than November 30, 1997. See back page ad for complete sweepstakes rules.

Celebrate with Love & Laughter™!

Official Entry Form

"Please enter me in the Love & Laughter Let's Celebrate Sweepstakes"

Name: _____

Address: _____

City: _____

State/Prov.: _____ Zip/Postal Code: _____

LLENTRY